MIND OF THE
MADNESS

MIND OF THE MADNESS

Talesa Jaramillo

JONES MEDIA
PUBLISHING

ISBN: 978-1-948382-21-2
JMP2021.2

To the memory of Mary Jaramillo.
Your strength and love has endured.

To my loving friends Jessica Alire and Kaua Lara.
Without your support, none of this would have been possible.
Thank you for always believing in me.

CONTENTS

CHAPTER ONE

IF I BELIEVED IN A god, I would have prayed for a different journey throughout my life. The means did not justify the end, but the end justified the means. This madness, it consumes through depletion and erosion. It desecrates your very senses and experiences. Though, I try, distinguishing this reality has fallen in vain.

A darkness looms through these walls here, flourishing in the fear of its inhabitants. It cannot be explained, only experienced. It comes unexpectedly, haphazardly, and with clear precision. The air is thick with the overbearing sense of suffocating fear. It is an earthly evil my words never will fully explain.

This sinister manifestation takes over every sense of your being, clouding your judgment and exhibiting in ways that are so real and clear yet feel contrived as illusions. Your eyes cannot be trusted. What you see cannot be believed, for it is not your mind playing tricks on you but another worldly force pulling you inward. Believe less in your weary eyes nor in what you can touch, for the world before you is . . . not.

Your soul reeks of a horror no man should encounter. The sights, the visits, will leave you paralyzed in dread. Time is but an illusion. There is no future or past. It just is. Or *was*. Atonement is delivered consciously and methodically. Every sin is remembered and relived. The fear is manifested, playing out right before your eyes. The previous life is shattered and the reality is gruesome, hopeless, and demented.

The lingering nights leave me to question my own sanity. Is what's before me real? When can I believe what I see or what I can touch? I must be going mad . . . . My mind aches from the mere fleeting moments of clarity. The enemy is no longer without. It is within. Evil exists. It is here. I have seen it. I am it. My mind wonders, *Has this darkness corrupted my inner being or has it only exposed who I have been so desperately trying to hide?*

What I have seen, felt, and heard, in these walls—the will to live lessens with each passing moment.

The incessant sound of drips of water, from the pipes above, fall to my bed, calming my racing mind. They nearly engulf the woeful cries emanating in the distance. With no way of telling time, I count each drop of water spilling to my bed. *One. Two. Three...* It is a welcome relief to know that time is still passing even when I feel motionless. But I keep tightly too, desperately holding on, though knowing there is nothing left to hold onto.

These concrete walls surrounding me are a cold, stark reminder of where I am, and where I'm *not*. This asylum seems older than hell itself, erected for the Devil's earthly pleasure. Solace is a fictious word in this world. "Abandon all hope ye who enter" is the perfect culmination of this unyielding hell. The words need to be etched in stone atop its entrance, a warning to those who enter . . . you may never truly leave.

More drops fall to my bed, soaking into the thin sheet I use to warm myself in these bitter nights. The curious drafts of wind are nearly unbearable. But are contrasted with the fleeting moments of sweat induced terror.

My belongings, my clothes, my humanity, it has all been stripped from me. The resounding thud of the judge's gavel was only the start. The chair was my sentence, but instead, I am here. I can remember uttering an insincere prayer to thank a god I did not believe in. But now, I curse it all.

My arrogance led me to believe that I was untouchable, incapable of being caught. But the more things stay the same, the more they *really* do change. I could not run on forever. The spotlight casted down its shining rays upon me, revealing who I was. And what I still *am*. But all the lights in the world could not illuminate the darkness I feel in my bones. It is lost. It is *all* lost.

A splash of water drips down my face, trailing to my empty hands, revealing the dearth. I have nothing to my name but that which surrounds me. A meager cot, which relishes in desecrating my back, gives way for endless, restless nights.

I can feel the bags growing heavy with each wipe of my eyes. Running my fingers through my oily, soft waves, I push back the hair bearing down on my face. My hands meet up to my eyes, catching way of the dirt building heavily in my fingernails, discoloring them beyond repair.

Hygiene is of no importance anymore. Long gone are the days of tailored suits, meticulously crafted onyx wavy locks, overpriced Rolex watches, carefully shined leather shoes, and a bare, clean-shaven face. An overgrown beard conceals my face, masking my infamous dimples that I once used to charm any ole dame.

Vociferous growls arise from the corner of this room. Curiously, light never reaches that area. It is allowed to stay hidden, concealed in darkness eternally. What lurks in obscurity never ceases to petrify me. Another chill engulfs the room, quickly reminding me to grab the damp blanket laying under my legs. Desperately, I wring out the blanket, praying for any semblance of warmth, wrapping it around my trembling body, never allowing my eyes to rise to the corner. The growl's voracity increases, but I never waver. My eyes are locked forward, spellbound in chills, concentrating on the chattering of my teeth. But the fear insists on building in my bones.

I long for an escape, any escape. To be free. But those words have always escaped me. My mind has always been chained down in its own confinement. Breaking through is my eternal life struggle. I await the day I break free. My soul is fraught in agony.

This cold, dark hell offers no comfort. The walls are thin in sound but too thick to escape. Squeezing my eyes shut, I try to drift to a different place, but the faint cries reverberate throughout my room pulling me back into this reality. A momentary sigh of relief falls from my mouth as my head falls back into the wall behind. Alas, the cries are from another and not me. The entity is terrorizing another, leaving me in solitude, for now.

But when the lights turn out, malevolence rises from below, dragging me deeper into its world. There is not a prayer that can be said to will me back. I am damned. But I am no longer sure I want to turn back.

My eyes are pulled from my dream state, lifting to the door only a few feet before me. The consecutive knocks disrupt my tranquil thoughts, quickening my heart rate, unsure what lies outside of this room. Through the cracks of my upheld fingers, I can see a figure descending toward me. My heart leaps out of my chest and into my throat, at a loss for words. My foggy eyes frenziedly fight for clarity, blinking rapidly in succession.

"Get up now, would ya?" Dick swats away my hand pulling on my arm, motioning for me to stand up. "The Doc wants to see ya soon. Get yerself washed up, *freak*." He furiously throws a towel at my face, catching at the top of my head, causing him to quietly chuckle. Slowly, I pull the towel from my face, glaring into his eyes. Pools of shit, they were, matching the words falling from his mouth. Staring at the towel in my hands, I can feel the coolness soaking into my dirty fingers. Using the towel, I clean my face and neck, then peer my eyes back up to Dick, wiping my mouth before throwing it back into his face. I could feel the smile etching into my face watching him become flustered.

Dick grips the towel, angrily throwing it to the ground. He rushes toward me, bending over to grab ahold of my collar, pulling me to eye level with him. The spit from his screams stirred on my face "Think y'er funny? Clean yerself up now!"

"I thought that's what I was doing." I smirked.

He pushed me back to the bed and quickly walked out of the room, slamming the door shut behind him.

The day will come when I will kill him. This is a promise.

He was known as an enforcer-type for Dr. Holmes. His most trusted right-hand man, despite his illiteracy and contrived bravado. Dr. Holmes's "special projects" are looked after by Dick, who has always been an asshole from the moment I entered this place. He seems to get off on it. But I can tell he has never handled one such as me. His insults and threats are meaningless hot air. He has yet to go through with his fits of anger. Deep inside, beneath that stocky frame, his ego has been shattered. I could kill him at any time, at any moment. And he knows this. How lucky he is that I cannot kill him, yet. If we were back in New York, his body would be at one with the earth by now.

Shaking my head in laughter, I stood, tucking my shirt into my trousers and straightening my collar. Out of the corner of my eye gleamed a metal bowl. Curiously, I walked toward it, bending down to examine the water inside. It was as clear as it could be with these rusty pipes. My eyes scanned the room, wondering when or how this bowl was brought in. But my chapped lips and dry mouth urged my hand to reach into it. Cupping the water in my hands, I brought the lukewarm water to my lips, slurping it in. I drank more and more, hoping to quench that yearning thirst. Nearly at the bottom, I used the last bit to splash onto my face and slick my hair back.

Without a towel, I dried my face on the bedsheet and sat back onto my bed, awaiting Dick's imminent return. The door opened revealing Dick's widened eyes as he was jostled by my presence. "Well, ya sure do look different when ya fix yerself up, now, don't ya?" he snarked. "Good then, let's go. You saved me a lotta energy and some mighty big problems if ya weren't." He leaned in to flash a grin at me, but I smoothly rose to my feet, erecting my shoulders, dusting myself off before meeting eye to eye. My chin lifted, stone-faced.

"I'm always ready. You can count on that. *Always*." I pressed forward, my shoulder knocking into his, sending him backward, barely gathering himself on the wall.

Catching his balance, he quickly stood and opened his mouth to yell, but my shoulders rose while my fists clenched tightly against my side. My eyes narrowed deeply, focused and ready for today to be that day. I could see the wheels in his mind turning, thinking better of his next reaction.

"Watch where ya going next time, ya hear?" He muttered, defeated.

"Sure. Sure I will."

Dick outstretched his right arm, motioning for me to lead the way. I obliged.

"After you." Dick said.

"Hmm." My head cocked back to examine him before continuing forward, entering into the narrow concrete-lined hallway. The lights gently flickered, mimicking a candle coming near the end of its wick. The tangy smell of sweat, urine, and agony filled into my nostrils. Drips of water falling from the cracks in the ceiling sat as a background noise to the pitter patter of my barefoot steps. We were not accommodated with shoes nor socks. At least I *wasn't*. My accommodations were rather sparse in all aspects.

With each step, my mind raced with thoughts of what was to come of me. Dr. Edward Holmes was unlike any physician I had been accustomed to. The man could have rightly fit in with any patient here, only his title lifting him from that burden.

He is a different type of evil. One I haven't quite figured out yet. I have met vile men. Many whom are dead now. But none of them intrigued me as he does. Just when I think I am coming to an understanding of who he is, his calming manner manages to disguise his hideous intentions. Nothing here is real. At least it seems. Even down to Dr. Holmes. There is something hidden beneath, longing to break through, to reveal its true self.

Each day I wonder why he has left me alive. So many failed experiments. Devastatingly painful treatments. All of which have brought me within inches of my death. And I cannot help but to wonder if I welcome this or still fear it. I still cannot discern how long I have been here . . . ?

"Keep up, Lyle. We got aways to go now, ya hear?" Dick's words echoed as if they were protruding from a distant room. He no longer sounded right behind me. My mind was wrapped in itself, dread pouring in heaps and loads.

Dr. Holmes's eerie face creeps into my thoughts, flashing his decrepit old smile. Something about him still sends chills down my spine. From our first meeting to what waits ahead, seeing him is a source of displeasure and inevitable pain.

The memory of meeting Dr. Holmes for the first time echoes in the darker parts of my mind. Apart from all the glitz and glamour and Hollywood-type faces, he had sat in the very back row of the courtroom—an elderly man whose visible giddiness had brought uneasiness to my spirit. Once the judge's gavel fell and I was sentenced, his abrupt "finally" turned heads and stirred judgments. My last memory as a free man is plagued by the vision of his wicked smile. "Soon" was all I could make out on his lips as I was led out of the courtroom in handcuffs.

Soon it was. Rikers was a mere rest stop before I was awakened in the middle of the night, forcibly taken from my cell and stuffed into a frozen paddy wagon. I imagined it would be better than death row. The electric chair seemed too final, morbid. But sometimes, quite possibly now, I tend to wish for quick finality instead of this slow agonizing death. My mind is deteriorating, one day at a time.

I remember seeing him on the steps of the asylum as we drove up on that chilly, fall night as the rain sliced through the air. Unbeknownst to me what awaited.

I was driven hours from my holding cell before we finally arrived. The distance was farther than I imagined, having me question if the coppers car would make it. I truly wish it hadn't.

As the asylum drew near, I can remember my body stiffening and my breath falling into a shallow pattern. This was not a hospital but an execution site for the castaways of the world.

The moonlight projected an ominous glow atop the castle-like building. We arrived in the desolate forest guarding the asylum. The reflection of the lights to the trees revealed its austere appearance. Within a stone's throw, you could see the rotting bark clutching tightly against the trees. A breeze mocked sinister crackling sounds as dead tree limbs rubbed swiftly against each other.

The sign outside the building was barely visible as it was nearly consumed by bushels of dying roses. The car rolled into a circular driveway as the rain slowed against the window.

Price State Institute.

The building itself is etched deeply within my mind. The medieval castle-like building seemed the hallmark of a desolate stench ridden hell trying to mask itself under cheap cologne. The aged black frost ashlar and large arch entrance provided a grand scale welcome to its prey. The exterior was engulfed by the surrounding elements. The size of the asylum was impressive but eerie. The columns traveled deep into the ground, running into hell, I'm sure. Windows were littered across the castle-like front. But the most menacing and, possibly, humiliating aspect was the giant clock tower at the helm of the building. It was like a mockery to those who would enter but never leave. You never really escape a place like this. Not even in death. It stays with you. Eternally. My stare fixated on the tower, waiting for the clock's hands to move, but they never did. The time was seemingly frozen at 3:00.

Dr. Holmes and others awaited outside. My focus was clearly on him. Even in the dark of night, his sinister smile beamed through. Clasping his hands together, he eagerly waited for the car to stop. His enthusiasm got the better of him as he hurried down the steps to the car, opening the backdoor himself. The fat man in front barely had time to turn off the engine.

"'*The Hangman of the Upper East*,' Mr. James Lyle . . ." A nickname I loathed. Nor understood. I only hanged one man, as I needed an out. I did not have my revolver, and the kill was opportune. It was not planned. But the papers needed a villain and the name aligned with their narrative. I was crucified in the papers. People I had never met testified false stories and misguided reasons to why I did what I did. Truth of the matter is, I liked it.

"Yes, yes! Welcome! Welcome *to your new home*, Mr. James Lyle! Or is it Lyle? I heard that was what you preferred, yes?" He had a peculiar Americanized English accent. I wish he would have stayed overseas.

"Mhmm," I muttered, examining him.

"Well then, I, myself, am Dr. Edward Holmes. The facilitator of this fine institute here." He turned and waved his right arm in the air, presenting the conspicuous building. "Beautiful, is it not? Spectacular in size. Glorious in architecture. And, and inescapable even right down to the *soul.*" He pointed at his chest but his eyes searched for fear in mine. "It is an absolute pleasure to meet you. I have heard so much about you."

"No moat?" *From the looks of this place, King Arthur could have resided here.*

"Pardon?" He leaned in as if he didn't hear the question.

"No moat?" I repeated.

"Moat? Oh, what a silly sense of humor you still have! Wonderful!" Dr. Holmes eagerly exclaimed with a joyful demeanor as he reached out his right hand to shake mine.

I looked down at his hand and lifted mine to show the cuffs that enclosed mine.

"Right. The handcuffs. Not to worry, not to worry, my dear. Those will be off soon enough!" He laughed as he pulled back his hand and joyfully clasped his hands together.

The instant rush of a tangy mold smell from the surrounding forest whipped across my face with the force of the wind. The unpleasantry was unexpected and unwelcomed. It immediately disarmed me but caused waves in my stomach. The chill was felt throughout my body, causing an uncontrollable tremble.

"Don't worry, Mr. Lyle, it's much warmer inside, I assure you. We won't be too much longer out here." Dr. Holmes looked to continue but by this time, the officer, Crowley, had waddled himself to the opened door and warned Dr. Holmes not to greet a convict without his presence.

"Nonsense! I have hundreds of patients here, all of which I am more than adept at handling. I *chose* him for God sakes man, did I not? Do you think I cannot handle a man such as him? Hmm? Do you, Mr. Crowley?" Dr. Holmes demanded, his frosty eyebrows raising to the top of his forehead.

"No . . . no, sir. This isn't what I was saying at all. I apologize regretfully. I overstepped my bounds, sir." Crowley's eyes met the floor as his head hung in shame.

In their heated arguments, I rose out of the car to view the new world surrounding me. *It's a Goddamn fortress.* My eyes drifted from the asylum to the impending growing storm returning above us. The sky grew darker, now replacing the moon's prior glow. The rain's ferocity returned but the storm melted into a meaningless backdrop to what I had before me. Dread filled my heart. My feet grew heavy, hoping to anchor my body into the mud to prevent entering. The wind's angry whispers raged to a cantankerous roar. My insides were burning, setting off alarms to avoid this place. I knew something was more than off. It is treacherous.

"Just get him up these damn steps and bring him inside! I have been dying to meet him! Now hurry up!" Dr. Holmes barked at the others.

My face fell to meet the other's behind Dr. Holmes as the rain pelted my back and my hair washed over my forehead. Three individuals impatiently stood under the arches, blocked from the assailing waters.

Crowley grabbed at my handcuffed arms and yanked me up the steps. My feet weighed down by the inches of mud dipped in my shoe. The smell of the air drifted into my nose sending aches down into my stomach. My eyes carefully examined each step to prevent a fall to the stone flooring. "Move it boy!" was all I remember as I felt a push from behind me.

The large black double doors swung open, revealing its capacious interior meeting with the foyer. I nearly slipped as I was pushed again by the fat man. My shoes were drenched with water and covered in mud as I slid across the glistening floors, hardly catching my bearings.

My eyes ogled at the gaudiness of what was supposed to be an asylum. The far-reaching endless windows were doorways to the soul of this place, seeing inside and outside of this labyrinth. The crystal chandelier hanging in the entrance set the room ablaze. An asylum seemed nowhere in sight.

From its exterior, I expected filth, clutter, and disruption, but was oddly met with unexpected peace and order. All my years I had believed an asylum to be rot with horrendous conditions, but the foyer of this place smashed all my misconceptions. It's medieval exterior fooled me. Timeworn and outdated had no place in this modernized art-museum-like front room. The wooden floors were seamless and the initial grand staircase boasted a lovely clock piece. Audacious paintings of naked men, women, ships on a scattered sea, and a perplexing eye-catching portrait of a man's face. Two sides of him, half of him, an elegant individual boasting luxurious clothing while the other half stripped away to reveal his interior. His skin looked as if it was melting off. His bones protruding, but beneath his exterior, he was hollow. Empty. I could not stop myself from staring. I was captivated. Undoubtedly, he was a horrifying sight to behold, but my eyes felt a drawing aura. It was my time to see this. His unsettling eyes looked as if he was returning the stare, eyeing me. His bleak black eyes drew a cold gaze sucking me in. Whispers started, circling around me. One of them could have been him.

"Lovely, isn't it, Mr. Lyle?" Dr. Holmes interjected, walking up to me, breaking my gaze. My eyes fell from the trance, staring down at this ghostly figure before me. I could not decipher which was the more frightening sight: this painting or Dr. Holmes?

His boney fingers pointed down to the floors.

"I have them shined weekly, and each artifact in here is delicately dusted and carefully taken care of. Many are from my explorations in Egypt, Africa, and many of my other destinations."

He pressed his hands together in a congratulatory manner revealing his crooked very-English yellowed teeth.

"You see, I am quite the collector of fine art, artifacts, amongst *other things.*"

He stopped to let the words sit there in the air before continuing.

"I have a taste for the finer side of life, as you may know *all too well.* Isn't that right? You were the assumed heir of Wallace's empire, before, well, his tragic untimely passing? Hmm? There is so much to that story I want to explore with you . . . Luckily, we have all the time in the world to do so, now don't we?"

Dr. Holmes sneered, his glasses lifting his arched eyebrows.

His words rang empty as I was still reeling from the painting. Eyes locked in on the painting. His eyes devouring me.

"Mr. Lyle? Are you still with us?"

Dr. Holmes snapped his fingers in front of my face, wanting to gain back my attention.

"Ah, yes! The two-faced man. One of my prized possessions. Seductive, isn't it? Something alluring about this painting. You know, I have noticed certain individuals seem to be drawn into it . . . I actually picked it up in Afri—" His voice faded as the indecipherable whispers picked back up, pulling me back to the painting.

There was something sinister and revealing about this painting. The more I was entranced, the more I noticed. It seemed to want to unravel itself to me. What I had believed to be black eyes were actually hazel with a hint of blue. The skinned portion did not present a stone face, but instead, a seamless frown. A tear was running down his left cheek. The man seemed to be weeping. He was locked, trapped in this painting, unable to break free. I could feel it. Who he was bound itself tightly into the painting. There was no way out.

"The doctor is speaking to you!" I felt a slap across the back of my neck to see the cop in a fighting stance, his baton at the ready now in his right hand.

"Mr. Lyle, it would serve you to cooperate here. It never does a person good to fight this place. Or me. You will never win. You will just be *consumed*."

I turned my head back to Dr. Holmes, cocking my head slightly to the right.

"Is that so, *Doctor*?"

"Oh, how glorious you truly are, Mr. Lyle! I absolutely adore a challenge! I cannot wait to learn more of you in our time together. However long that may be!"

His dead blue eyes alerted me to something more devious. Watching him rub his palms back and forth as his glasses fell to the bridge of his large nose was unsightly. Age was not kind to him. His graying hair had nearly seeped back into his skull and the crow's feet only grew with each passing minute.

"Hmph."

Was all I could mutter. I was trying to read into him. He was tough. He seemed eccentric and fearless. Charismatic, really. Deceiving but captivating. Courteous and malicious. I was not sure if I hated or respected him yet. Time was yet to tell.

"I can personally guarantee that I—well, we—will take great care in aiding and treating your mental condition. I'm always on the cutting edge looking for the latest and greatest breakthrough for my patients, at *any* and *all* costs. Rest assured, Mr. Lyle, you are in the best of hands. Now, Richard, please get Mr. Lyle here settled in. It's been a long, hard drive, and I'm sure he is wanting to get out of these wet clothes. And have someone clean up this mess. There are mud tracks on my floors."

Dr. Holmes nodded then turned to walk away.

A splash of water hit my forehead from the pipes above, bringing me back to reality. I wiped the drop that landed on my brow, getting lost in the seemingly brighter lights above. *Dear Lord, I really am here, aren't I?*

CHAPTER TWO

"COME ON NOW! MOVE IT!"

Dick gripped my shoulder firmly, feeling the sting of his fingers against my skin. My eyes fell from the lights as the hallway's never-ending sights came clearly into view.

"Move it now before I make ya!"

The violent push nearly had me falling over my feet. I regained my composure and stepped forward. The lighting returned to a faintness, creating an uneasy feeling as a draft pushed up through my shirt, landing on my neck. Chills sprung up as my heart's pace steadily increased. My steps echoed thuds against the floor as the hall was unusually quiet. I scanned the passing rooms, searching for my friend Tommy, but darkness masked the trivial windows.

The halls felt endless, confusing, and directionless. It's as if it was done with intent. Without Dick guiding me, I'm not so sure I would find my way back. Or forward.

My bare feet were growing weary pattering against the cold and wet concrete floors. It felt as if we were walking for hours, endlessly falling into loops of uncertainty. Isolated in my room for so long, my feet have forgotten what it feels to walk such great lengths. Though, my legs are enjoying the physical activity, the soles of my feet are yearning for a rest.

"How much further?" I interrogated.

We had to be close. For both of our sakes.

"Eager now to meet the Doc?"

He half-chuckled before I snapped my head back narrowing in on him.

"We are almost there. Not too much further."

He tried to reassure, seeing my patience wearing thin. We nearly met eye to eye but he halted in his tracks. The creases on his forehead reflected his worry as his left hand lifted to brandish the truncheon.

"Keep moving. We're close."

My eyes dipped to look at his weapon, watching the veins protrude from his hands as he tightly gripped it. I audibly scoffed, turning away from him, deadpanned.

"Stop!" Dick yelled as we reached a metallic door. Unlike mine, there was no opening to look through.

"We enter in through here, and ya need to wait, Doc will be in soon, understand now?"

He eyed me, waiting for an answer, but I stood in silence. Something was off. A strange feeling rose up in the pits of my stomach. I wasn't sure what it was, unfamiliar, but it made me uneasy. I balled my clammy hands to avoid them from being seen. Dick opened the door, grabbed me, pushing me in before slamming the door shut. He did not follow.

I was engulfed in darkness. Turning back toward the door, my hands searched the wall for the doorknob, hoping to exit the room, unsure of what was to come. Perplexed, there was no knob to be found. I felt every piece of where the door was, nothing was to be found.

I outstretched my arms, looking for another exit. *Maybe I missed it? Has to be here somewhere.*

Judiciously, my steps were shallow. The room seemed never-ending. A frigid wind blew, increasing its voracity, blaring unbearably freezing chills at my feet. My toes curled into the concrete, uncomfortable. The temperature in the room was falling at the speed of lightening. My breaths shallowed. The room's air whipped tightly across my chest with every breath stinging violently.

Obscenities littered my mind's thoughts. I could not think of a plan, a next step. Survival was, now, the only necessity.

Just as my eyes were adjusting to the dark, an overbearing ray of light beamed down from above, blinding me. My hands shot up to shield the blinding rays. The light sent my pinched eyes into a stream of tears. The strength in my legs curiously weakened, causing me to drop to my right knee. Hoping for a reprieve, I buried my face into my thighs facing toward the ground. The brightness set the rooms temperatures ablaze. The rapid succession of frigid temperatures into unwavering heat sent my body into a spiral, reeling in chills but, now, sweating in heaps.

My hands clenched into my hair. "What is this?" I bellowed.

A distant low-growl answered. Everything stopped. My mind's thoughts were quelled, the blinding lights, everything fell to the wayside under the unmistakable sound. The malevolence rang true, surrounding me wholly, pinning my body into the ground. I could not move.

It was unlike any sound I have heard before. The hair on my arms shot up while my heart beat against my ribcage. My shallowed breathing returned. What could I make of that sound? It was profound and callous. My mind quickly tried to reason against it. The sound would not exist if I didn't accept its existence.

I flung my hands to my ears to obscure the returning sound, but it grew even louder. It no longer sounded distant, but instead, as if it had situated itself within my mind. The sound was maddening. Its volume increasing, my thoughts were filled with only this. I punched at the concrete floor, but the blare infected my head. The pulsing pain of my bleeding knuckles did not deter the sound. It bit at me, striking with episodic feats of roars. Low growls, high screams, they were various and random. I could feel my mouth dropping to yell over the sounds. But I was inaudible. The crescendo built. I grasped even tighter at my hair, ready to tear the sound out of my head if need be.

Then it ceased. All at once. The room drifted into an eerie silence as a sense of warmth rushed over me.

I cautiously allowed one lid to open, unsure of what I would see. The blaring light had dimmed to the shadow of a fires ember. The crinkling of embers and the smell of fresh pine ruminated in the air. My hands fell in relief to my sides, exhausted from the tension they were under. Exhausted, I dug my palms into the floor and fought to sit my weakened body up, aghast to feel dirt underneath my feet. My scanning eyes paused to gape at what surrounded me. And *who*.

"Get up, Lyle, let's dance!"

My mother, towering above me outstretched her hand to lift me from the floor. My eyes shot open in bewilderment.

How could this be? This must be a dream. This has to be a dream. Wake up Lyle. Wake up!

I smacked my right hand at my cheek, hoping I would awake. But Clara stood, perplexed, grabbing my arm, stopping me from continuing.

"Come on, silly, we haven't much time before your father comes home. Let's dance!"

Her sweet tone calmed my disillusioned senses, allowing me to grab her hand. We walked toward the window as she turned to walk to the gramophone. Observing every detail of the room, I did not know what to make of the moment. None of this seemed real, it couldn't be.

Her favorite song, "Come Josephine in My Flying Machine," started up, startling me; I narrowed my gaze back to Clara. I hadn't heard this song in ages. I haven't wanted to.

The song's melody drifted to the background as my wandering eyes fell upon my mother. The moon's glow danced over Clara's smile, beaming through. I couldn't help but return the smile. This image of her is the one I always keep. Young, alive, and radiant. It has been decades since I have seen her last. My memories of her have drifted over the years, but she still remains the most beautiful woman I have ever seen.

She grabbed my hand and lifted my arms, "You can't have stringy arms, Lyle. You have to be confident. Brave. Bold."

She smiled and lifted my drooping chin.

"Bold."

She sweetly reassured as we danced around the dirt floor, her blue dress discoloring from the flying spats of dirt. The light captured her just seamlessly. Her beauty always radiated when she smiled. She was not destined to be trapped inside a loveless marriage; no, this woman could have been a star. But the life in her was fading, year by year. I'm sure this is why I have never returned for her. I want to picture her just this way. Perfect, confident, and glowing with ease.

Clara should have been in theatre or the big screen, perhaps the leading role, not trapped here in a dilapidated wooden house. She should be out there. Doing so much more. Capturing the hearts of men with her hourglass figure, voluminous wavy chestnut-brown hair, plump red lips, and olive skin. She was destined for greatness, not the whore house she eventually found herself in.

She longed to fly from this reality. I looked up from my awkward footing to see her happily singing along. Her voice was that of the angels. I had nearly forgotten her tone. The sound quickly sunk into my ears as I tried to soak it in. I remember her voice always being there, even in the most difficult moments. I stared back at her, my smile never leaving my face. I cannot remember the last time I smiled as I am. Her lips continued to the song, turning to me at times, flashing those perfect teeth.

"Focus sweetie. I can't afford bruised toes now!"

She gently smacked at the side of my shoulder as we continued, twirling her around the floor, creating winds of dirt. We were both lost in the moment. I did not want it to end.

Then the door rushed open. And *he* was there. The smell of whisky and tobacco quickly filled the room. It's stench was unmistakable.

Jim drunkenly stumbled through the doorway. He dropped the bottle of whisky in the dirt, throwing him in a fit of rage as it seeped into the thirsty ground. He quickly snatched the bottle into his left hand and guzzled what was left.

"That's a damn shame, a no good, rotten shame!"

He stared at the empty bottle in his hand letting out a vulgar belch. His dilated eyes drifted onto us while the music continued to play in the background.

"What a Goddamn shame ya two are."

He chucked the bottle at the gramophone, causing it to fall over and bust on the ground.

"God damn it, Jim! You . . . you always do this!"

Tears welled in Clara's eyes as she rushed over to pick up the gramophone. I looked over to see her broken spirit melting into the floor as she gripped the pieces of the shattered record into her chest.

"I pay for it, don't I? Don't I?" He bellowed. "All of this, every goddamn thing in this house, it's all *mine*. All of it! And that includes the both of yer."

He pointed at Clara and then drunkenly swayed his finger toward me. My smile had been replaced with a scowl. My hands clenched into a tight fist, the veins nearly protruding out of my arms.

"Oh, what boy? Think your tough now, do ya? Ya want to take a shot at yer old man now? Well come on, free shot right here. Come on!"

He leaned his cheek forward, motioning for me to come toward him. But I didn't, I stood there glaring back at him.

"Didn't ya hear me, boy? Those tight fists ya have there, well lay one on me. Come on now! Don't be a coward now, do it! Do it now!"

He screamed, spit flinging out of his mouth. But I still did not react, I couldn't. My feet were planted in the ground. I was unable to move, unable to talk even as the fury raged inside of me. He stumbled his way toward me, grabbing my fist and lifted it up to his face. I looked up to see him looming over me. His green eyes always seemed to fade into a black during his drunken stupor.

"My boy, a Goddamn coward. Who woulda thought? Me, a fighter as a young boy. Afraid of absolutely no one. Not a goddamn thing. But you here, junior, a girly boy. I raised ya too soft now, didn't I? Huh? Too fucking soft!"

A smack whipped harshly across my face. The impact prompted a burst of blood to rush through my mouth as I had bit my tongue.

"Come on, boy, hit me!"

Another smack blistered my cheek, staggering me back. My eyes watered as my right cheek ached in pain.

"Leave him alone, Jim!" Clara interjected as she hastily stood up.

"Shut up woman! Or I'll go over there and deal with you!"

He turned his wretched face back to mine, scrutinizing me.

"Are ya crying now, ya girly boy? Huh, are you crying?" he mocked. "I need to toughen ya up, make a real man out of ya, like me!"

A familiar blow hit my stomach as I dropped to the ground. The taste of dirt gathered in my mouth while more blows nailed my throbbing body. My stomach was overwhelmed, forcibly coughing to find a reprieve.

In my periphery, I could see Clara running up to Jim and pulling his hair.

Don't touch—

He turned around and smacked her to the ground. She fell back to the dirt, clutching at her face as he lifted her up one more time to belt another smack her way. She screamed in pain, lumps of tears cascading down her cheek.

A rush of anger garnered a bit of strength in my aching body as I attempted to stand, but Jim was quick to meet my stance and whipped me across my back with his belt he had pulled from his trousers. The buckle bounced across my back sending shock waves as he pummeled me into the ground. I felt a warm liquid run down my lower back as my head grew weary. Jim turned me on my back and stood over me. His figure drew distant as my eyes blurred. He dropped to his knee and lifted my head, moving his face closer into mine, mouth ready to roar in anger.

"Mr. Lyle, Mr. Lyle! Wake up! Can you hear me? Mr. Lyle, say something so I know you hear me."

The sound of the voice cleared as I opened my eyes to reveal Dr. Holmes kneeling before me, lifting my throbbing head.

CHAPTER THREE

MY EYEBROWS ROSE AND MY eyes widened, *is this real*? Needing to know, I reached for Dr. Holmes, but my hands were quickly smacked down by Dick.

"Don't even think about it!"

Thoughts burst through my head, racing at the speed of light. My eyes purposely scanned the surroundings, failing to blink. A stone-faced expression settled, trying not to give way to the confusion. Dr. Holmes's eyes studied my face, trying to read what wasn't being said. Feeling the weight of his judgment, I motioned to situate myself on my arms, wanting to sit up, but my stomach felt a familiar ache. I let out an exasperated breath, dropping my head, reeling in agony. Throbbing internal mounds lit up my insides, having me clutch at my abdomen area. Aghast at the onset of the pain, I carefully lifted my shirt revealing purple discoloring painted across my ribs. Horrified, I flung my shirt back down, but Dr. Holmes's had taken noticed.

"Peculiar . . . Now, how could that have happened? An odd pattern there, yes?"

He pressed firmly on the bruising sending shockwaves of pangs. I struck his hands off and scooted from him.

"Peculiar, indeed. How did you manage this? Take off your shirt, I need to see the full extent of the injuries."

I could feel my eyes growing over three sizes. *This doesn't make sense. It cannot be real. It was just a dream . . .*

"Mr. Lyle, please. Please cooperate."

I was snapped back to reality.

"I would hate to have to ask you another time. Now please, the shirt?"

He reached out his hand, awaiting the shirt. But my mind was lost in disbelief.

A striking electricity of pain erupted from my lower back as I felt Dick rush behind me, jerking me up from the floor, ripping the shirt from my back. I bellowed out in pain, desperately clutching at my back, feeling a warm liquid trailing down. I brought my shaking hands to my face to see the vibrant red layered on my fingers.

Dear God!

"Well, well, Mr. Lyle. Quite the peculiar one, indeed. What to do, what to do?"

Dr. Holmes peered down, examining my spine.

"This will need to be cleaned up. Yes, indeed. Let's take him to the medical office, I can treat his wound."

Dr. Holmes's motioned for me to follow as we exited the room into the hallway. My mind was racing, trying to gather my thoughts.

Did I take a hard fall? Was I attacked? Dick? That son of a bitch! It must've been him, there is no other explanation. Unless, unless I'm still dreaming now? Am I dreaming? I'm losing my Goddamn mind in here . . .

"Ah, here we are, Mr. Lyle, go ahead, please enter."

Dr. Holmes opened the door and proceeded to walk through, turning to ensure I complied.

"The gurney right there, please, sit."

The gurney had remnants of dry blood splatter on the wheels, unsettling enough. Dick pushed me from behind, sending strikes of needle-like pricks down my spine. I clenched my teeth hoping to mask my discomfort. A tear gathered at the corner of my eye, but I wiped it quickly to ensure it was hidden from view.

Son of a bitch. The pain was nearly unbearable with each step. Finally, I made it to the gurney just as Dr. Holmes arrived back in the room with his medical kit.

"Alright, now, let me see here. Ah, yes, I'll need to clean this up to prevent it from getting infected, you see, and then I'll bandage you right up. You'll be good as new. Though, this *will hurt*. Temporarily, of course."

A smile nearly cracking through his demented face.

Taking inventory of my wounds, Dr. Holmes circled me, but my attention was elsewhere. Dr. Holmes's taste for "art" never failed to make me uneasy. Jars of body parts emerged in water: eyes, hearts, and brains. He is the crazy one. His awards from various groups and medical advancements were scattered boastfully on the wall. *Achievements in breakthrough medical achievements, what a sick joke.*

In the corner of the room, facing back at me was a slack-jawed skeleton. The eyes, however, remained fully intact, disturbingly so. In the light, they seemed a dull gray. Everything here seemed to leer back at me. My stare must have been pronounced as I was caught staring at it.

"Incredible, isn't it? The human body, so fascinating! What it can *withstand*, absolutely remarkable! It *is real*, I assure you."

Fits of a fury stung harshly from the wound treatment, distracting me from the skeleton man and pushing me to leap to my feet. A desperate muffled scream loomed from my mouth as I took my fist against the concrete wall. I shook my hand in discomfort as the incineration nearly engulfed all of my senses.

"Mr. Lyle, you need to sit back down. I am not finished. It will be uncomfortable, as I had previously addressed, but it needs to be treated! *Now sit!*"

Dick walked up to grab me, but I raised my finger up to his face, glaring at him.

"Don't even think of it!"

Dick backed away, hands raised, allowing me to sit back on the gurney. My hands attempted to rip through the metal as nearly every second was intolerable. My veins looked ready to burst out of my skin.

"Please calm your body, Mr. Lyle. The trembling is making it difficult to wrap accurately," Dr. Holmes snapped.

Unbeknownst to me, my body was violently shaking from the pain. Hoping to calm myself, I practiced taking deep inhales and exhales, praying my focus would turn elsewhere. I found myself staring at another one of his grandiose paintings. But this one was . . . odd. It felt as if it was moving in real time. A man standing under a streetlight on the corner of a street. At first he was crowded by passersby, but slowly the traffic waned and his face came into view. It was . . . me. He—well, I—was waving at myself. I swear I could hear him, yelling for me to join him. His words sounded so clear but ominous, "Come, Lyle! Come!"

"Ah, all better!" Dr. Holmes patted me on the back, pulling my gaze to his. "You do be careful now. Wouldn't want to make this any worse, now, would you?"

I let out a deep sigh, trying to breathe through my sore state. Dropping to the floor from the gurney, I grabbed at my body but thought better of it, instead, standing as best as I could, turning to look back at the painting. *Where? It's gone?* To my horror, the painting had disappeared. An empty space on the white block wall looked back at me. No sign of a painting having ever been hung there. *It was there. I know it was. Right there!* The unsettling urging words of the man in the painting still lingered in unison for a brief moment, before vanishing as quickly as the painting did.

"What an improvement—"

Dr. Holmes interjected my thoughts.

"Here, take a look at the work, quite remarkable work, don't you say?" He lifted a mirror to an unrecognizable image.

Is that . . . is that me? A few white strands blended into my black hair. The bags under my eyes resembled pillows as my face looked swollen. A deep redness obscured my viridescent eyes. The fullness of my neck had been narrowed thin. *Christ, I look exactly like Jim.*

"I'm afraid we will have to postpone our session today, Mr. Lyle. I have pressing matters to attend to, please forgive me. I know I will see you soon enough. I do look forward to it, as I always do!"

Dr. Holmes quickly walked out of the room into the hallway. Dick approached, throwing a new shirt at me.

"Throw this on. Now back to the room ya go!"

He reached to grab my shoulder, but I rolled my arm back scowling at him.

"Move then!" He snapped.

I moved toward him, coming face-to-face as I felt his uneasiness. I stood there for a few seconds, without a blink and devoid of a facial reaction. He stepped back and waved his hand to the door as I smirked and obliged.

Walking into my room as the door eagerly shut behind me, I was reminded of the striking pain in my back. The pain was quick and subtle, a warning that its power was overwhelming and fierce.

CHAPTER FOUR

I SPRANG UP FROM MY bed, sweat beading across my forehead and heart pounding out of my chest, relieved to be awake. *It was just a dream.* A vicious nightmare, that felt all too real, faded into the background. Gritting my teeth to muffle my eager cries, I felt a burning sensation glide up my lower back to the top of my neck. My hands sunk into the bed, desperately gripping the sheets around me into a clenched fist. My thoughts, my fears, all quelled under the ferocious strain.

A breath of light made its way under my door, catching the attention of my wide eyes. Unexpectedly, the pain ceased, all at once, the burning dissipated. My tense body fell to a hunched position as I curiously looked at the fragment of light. A tray of food and a cup was placed on the ground in view of the light.

Quickly, I rushed over and grabbed the tray, devouring the food as quickly as I could, awakening my stomach in hunger. My dry mouth pleaded for a taste of water, thankful when I lifted its contents to my cracked lips, drinking all I could handle before returning to the bread and rice dish. Once the food was consumed and the water drunk, I sat back, staring at the empty tray.

What have I become?

I leaned my head back against the wall, ashamed. I have become exactly what I have feared, the shell of the man I once was.

A shadow washed over my face from the hallway's dim light. I wondered who was out there, outside of my door. My soul longed for something, someone. The time here has felt endless, drawn on without having Tommy in the room next to me.

When I first arrived, Tommy was in the room to my right, he had arrived some time before me and had more of an understanding of the place. The first night I arrived, I was plagued with horrific nightmares, my screams forcing me awake.

"Oh boy, another screamer we have here." A lighthearted chuckle penetrated through the walls. "Ya'll be alright, mate. Ya'll get used to it." Tommy yelled.

Unsure what to make of his words, I laid silently in bed, my rapid heart rate assuring me I was still alive.

"The name's Tommy. Tommy Lancaster. Proper Englishman as ya can tell. Where abouts you from?" His voice sounded unobstructed. As if he was here in the room with me. At first it was unsettling, but the more he spoke, the more I relished in the company.

"Giving me the silent treatment there, mate? Weird fella. Yer that new one, that murderer from New York? Am I right?"

How could he possibly know this?

"Ah mate, we don't have to talk about it if you don't wanna. Just trying to be friendly is all. Yer gonna need a proper friend in here. I can guarantee ya that. Anywho, I'm Tommy, again. I'm not going anywhere, so feel free to speak when yer mouth decides to open." He giggled.

"How—how do you know this?" was all I could mutter, indecisive about his intentions.

"Ha, mate, it's not a secret. Been reading about ya in the papers for years. Killing a bunch of posh wankers? Good for you! Too many of those evil rich bastards anyhow."

"I made the papers in England?"

"No mate. Don't get too big of a head now, no. I moved to New York some time back and I read about ya. Then I overheard the Doc saying they were gonna put a high profile killer in the room next to me. Connected the dots. Pretty smart fella, you will come to see. Ha! Not too many blokes with the fancy name of, what was it, 'The Hangman of the Upper East'? Now that's a real proper name. Fancy that?"

"No. It's pure fiction."

Knowing the papers painted me as some maniacal killer inflamed me. These men weren't really men, they were the scum of the earth. Abusers. Liars. Cheats. All of whom just so happened to have heaps of money in front of their names. Yes, I killed them. But there is a piece of me that is uncontrollable, insatiable. But I would never kill the defenseless, the vulnerable. Not as the papers made me out to be.

"It's a great name mate, be proud."

"Well don't go believing all you have read. It's mostly bullshit."

"No judgment from over here, mate. I can't exactly judge you when I'm talking on the other side of the same wall, now, right?" Tommy chuckled.

His laugh was contagious, loud and wheezy. It lifted a smile onto my grimaced face. His wittiness is not what I would have expected in this dreary place.

"Tommy, huh? Why are you here? What did you do?" I posed, genuinely intrigued.

"Ya mean, did I kill someone too? Or am I batshit crazy? Want to see if yer talking to a psycho now?"

"Well, naturally."

"I'm not crazy, mate, just built different, I s'pose."

"That's what they all say, right?"

"It would be easier if I was mad. Believe me. This all would."

The tone of his voice fell into a near despair. I could tell there was something deeper under the surface of his lighthearted humor.

"Are you in here for the long haul?"

"Ya know, mate, I really don't know. It all seemed to happen so fast. One minute I was out there, living life. Then words were said, rumors spread, and I sorta ended up here. Ya know, don't go believing all that's said about ya, right?"

"Right . . . But what is it? Something worse than murder?"

"Nah, mate. But sometimes I wish I did, ya know? For all that happened and how I got here, it would've been easier. But it's a long story. Can get me quite worked up."

"Well . . . I don't seem to be going anywhere. Time's kind of on my side. And I have nothing else to do, from the looks of it, neither do you. So regale me."

Tommy told me of his time in New York and how he fell in love with the wrong person. Unfortunately, for him, the man was the son of a prominent New York senator. Tommy and his lover, Ralph, were spotted together at the Renaissance Casino in Harlem attending a masquerade, as well as other public places throughout the state.

His voice lit up when speaking about Ralph, "We knew it was wrong but we didn't care. We were carefree and in love. We had to take a chance, ya know?"

But the relationship leaked into the papers, causing a rising scandal for the senator.

"He called us perverts and fags. His own son, can you believe it? Threatening to disown him, quash his inheritance, all of it. And then, then he beat him in the living room with me right there. I cried out to him, held back by his goons."

But even with Tommy's adamant pledges to keep the relationship a secret and to stay clear of Ralph until after the election, the senator called in a few favors and had Tommy committed.

"What happened to Ralph, Tommy?"

"I never heard from him again . . ."

He let the words sit there for a few breaths, trying to regain his composure.

"But I still think of him, every day, in fact, and I pray he's all right. Lyle?"

"Erm?"

"You ever met anyone like me?"

"What? A cripple?" I sarcastically laughed.

"Ya know yer some kind of asshole. No, a gay man?"

"You ever met a murderer?"

"Ah, you got me there mate."

"I don't like to assume things about people, I'd prefer if you didn't either. You seem alright from what I can tell."

"Lyle, did you really murder as many people as they say?"

"How many did *they say*?"

"Quite the lot."

"You know, it all blurs for me. I know it happened, but it's as if someone else was in control, and I was watching. From the sidelines, ya know? Something just takes over and a switch is hit. I become someone else, *something* else."

"Think you'll kill again?"

I let the words sit. Even I was unsure of the answer.

"Ah, well, you seem better than the last guy, he was a proper nut. Real loon."

"What happened to him?"

"His name is Lockeheart. They moved him across the hall a few doors down."

"Oh yeah, what's so crazy about him?"

"He murdered his entire family. Shot them all dead. Right there in the house. But went on for months without telling a soul. He kept them all right where they were too, never moved the bodies. Just went about his business."

"How'd they catch him?"

"His wife's mother came to pay an unexpected visit while he was in town. Heard the house's smell was unbearable. Several Bobbie's were proper sick. It was all over the papers. A couple years back. It was pretty big, well, until you."

"Hmph. Must've missed it, then. You know, being the evil man they painted me out to be."

"Maybe you aren't as bad as the papers make you out to be."

"Tommy?"

"Yeah?"

"How'd you end up in that chair anyway?"

"Oh this, this is new." He half-heartedly laughed.

"Once the whole world knows you are different, ya can bet they will do everything they can to quash you. I'm lucky to have survived. Well . . . maybe not, since I'm locked away here, talking to ya."

His sense of humor returned with his belly laugh.

"Did you know them?"

"No . . . I was hit over the head first. Woke up days later in the hospital. My life spun from there and now I'm here."

I caught myself leaning my head against the concrete wall opposite of where Tommy was, saddened that life thrusted its vengeful hammer on him as well.

"Just don't go falling in love with me, deal?"

Our laughter temporarily broke the solemnity surrounding us. The echo filled the space of the empty room giving me a sense of hope that even in this dark hell, there may be some light, even if only temporary.

CHAPTER FIVE

THESE ENDLESS DAYS, ALONE, RIDDLED in pain, are unyielding. Time stands frozen. Each hour passes, but it all feels the same. Staring at the walls around me, I have counted nearly every chip and crack within them. The scratches and chipped portion tell a story I would be interested in knowing.

My mind wanders gazing into the darkness, of what could have been and what was. Sometimes my mind wanders to Charles. The years spent with him, the only real father I had known, sheltering me, educating me, the places I had seen with him, and the people we met, are now haunting memories of a past I cannot fix.

Rubbing my fingers across my bruised left wrist, I remembered the watch he had given me. A slight smile dug its way onto my face. The tailored suits, large gala parties, fancy dinners, and endless amounts of cash were trivial to others but extraordinary coming from my humble upbringing. I had never experienced such a rich and full life until he took me under his wing. Thinking of him cuts at me, internally, but I treasure the years I had as I had never met a man so intent on never living a normal life.

Powerful, rich, vivacious, cunning, lustful, insatiable, and above all else, ruthless. That's what Charles was. I respected him. I looked up to him.

He was the only real father figure I had. He tried to save me, to fix me. I wish he had. Without him, I would've given up completely.

Having left home, the mean streets of New York offered no solace to a young child like me. Living alone and destitute taught me to fight, but deep down, I was becoming weary. My soul was fading. It seemed as if life was nothing more than an unwinnable fight against a rising tide. It was near too much. I needed something more, something different. *Someone.*

The first time I had seen Charles was in the alleyway of L'Aiglon, a local French restaurant. I studied him for days, watching as he would enter and exit the restaurant alone. I was considering robbing him, desperate, hungry, and at my wits' end.

The restaurant owner found me eating from the trash bin and threatened to have me arrested if I didn't leave. Food was scarce already and I needed the means to get more.

Charles paraded himself, flaunting off his exuberant wealth, begging to be robbed. His attire was pompous but stylish. I envied his three-piece fitted suits, his signature panama hat, and leather bound shoes. He never wore the same outfit twice. Money dripped from his fingers. I wanted this, too.

The violent pangs of hunger whipped some courage into me. I surprised him from behind, holding a club I had stolen, threatening him to hand over everything he had. But his reaction was curious. It was as if he had been through this before. He laughed, throwing up his hands and jokingly uttered, "Don't hurt me now." I lifted the club to assert my intentions, but my stomach pangs were audible, quelling the moment. He dropped his arms and searched in his pocket pulling out a few rolls of cash. My eyebrows lifted near to the top of my forehead. I had never seen that much money in all of my life.

"Here, here's a couple of dollars. Get you a hot meal, a shower, and a set of new clothes. If you need more, well, you seem to know where to find me."

He lifted up my left hand and placed the money in, closing my fist ensuring I held onto it.

"Oh, and kid, next time, don't bring the bat, alright?" He grinned then walked to the alleyway door of the restaurant, whistling as he entered.

Each week I would stop by the alleyway and wait for him and as he promised, sparing me a few dollars. But he took inventory, wanting to know all I had spent it on. Buying food was my priority and avoiding being robbed, which had happened the first week. After the fourth week, he stopped giving me money.

"Now kid, I told you to buy some decent clothes. Look at you, you're a mess and you smell like hell."

I didn't know what to say. I hung my head, my chin drooping into my chest.

"What's your name, kid?"

I looked up at him, but I was afraid to answer. I continued kicking the rocks against the wall.

"I'm Charles, Charles Wallace. Do you see the end of this alleyway? Well if you head down it about a block or so, I work down there. I'm a lawyer, taking care of rich people's money and the sort. Now, I can see that you are leery of me and I won't pretend to know why. But I can't seem to trust you to buy some decent clothing with the money I have been giving you. You still look a mess."

My head fell further down in shame. He knew his words stung me.

"Around the corner here is a barber shop, a good one." He pointed. "They will take good care of you. Follow me there and then we will get you some proper clothes. You have more holes in your clothes than a block of cheese. And those shoes. How do you walk in them? No matter, just follow me, understand?"

I watched him as he walked forward, turning back to see if I'd follow. I took a few steps when he wasn't looking, then would stop; I was leery, wanting to maintain a distance in the event I needed to run. But he was patient, he didn't insist nor scream. And as he promised, we ended up at the barber shop where I was cleaned up. The barber must've been familiar with Charles because he asked the man in the chair to get up and make way for me. He didn't even charge Charles, telling him it was "on the house."

Charles graciously thanked him and we exited, heading to the nearest clothing store. I was bought new clothes and a brand new pair of shoes. I had never worn new shoes, not my own. The one's I had on my feet I had lifted from a smaller boy walking down the street, but they were worn and aged. I felt terrible but I needed some comfort for my aching feet.

To him, the money spent was a typical Tuesday afternoon, but to me, it meant the world. I had to look down at the floor so he couldn't see my welled up eyes. He caught sight of it for a minute but quickly turned away. He knew I was embarrassed and didn't want to add to it.

He offered to take me out to lunch, knowing I hadn't eaten. I couldn't help but to accept. I had never been inside of a fancy restaurant. The food was surprisingly even tastier fresh then it was from the garbage.

The first few minutes were quiet. I could see the lines of his forehead wrinkle, watching him study me, trying to take a read into who I was.

"Quiet kid, aren't you?"

I raised my shoulders and continued looking around at the majesty of the place, the smells, the people, all of it was bewildering and breathtaking.

"Well, since you aren't much of a talker, you can sit and listen to me. I have quite the endless stories."

He regaled me of stories of his past days in the navy, entering into law, and the people he had met, including Babe Ruth, which had my full attention.

"It's Lyle."

I finally told him. I could see his eyes perk up as he ordered us dessert.

Every day, instead of giving me money, we would meet for lunch and he would tell me a little more about him each time. A piece of me enjoyed this, but I hushed it inside. I was too afraid. But he never gave up. I think he enjoyed it too. He had, recently, lost his wife and their baby. He was alone. I think he needed this too.

In the restaurant, the respect he commanded in the room, any room, was powerful; it was visible. Men would go out of their way to offer assistance or to let them know he was welcome. But even in all the respect and admiration, he never took it to heart.

"These men in here, all the men who come up to me and try to make nice, they want something. Maybe not now, but eventually they will. And it can cost you. Be sure you know who you are dealing with. Always. Never make the mistake of underestimating someone because they just might be the ones shoving the knife into your back."

He told me of how he grew up dirt poor and had to fight his way up the ladder. Cutthroat business deals were a way of life.

"Business isn't about doing what's right for someone else, it's about what's right for you. Take all you can from them until they have nothing more to offer. Exhaust it all then bow out. And make as much money as you can. You can buy much with it. People. Power. Everything. Remember, it's all business in the end. This comes first, before people, before family. Before anything. Always. Understand?"

Having come from nothing, hearing about the wealth he had and the arrogance he portrayed, I was hooked. Little by little, I began to tell him of my life, where I had come from and the beatings I endured from Jim. The lunches were more than conversations, they were tokens of wisdom and opportunities. After months of meeting, he offered me a position to work under him at his practice.

Different men would walk in each day with suitcases of cash and walkout empty handed. Where to place the money was Charles's specialty. He ensured the rich remained powerful, free of burdensome taxes, while lining his pockets with untraceable bills. The work was a drug, and I, an addict.

The days turned to years, my wallet lined, my clothes bared names I barely knew how to pronounce, and my nights involved a plethora of numerous women. Charles educated me in not only financial laws but in negotiating, deals, and reading people. Understanding how someone will react before they even open their mouths is key to finalizing a deal on your terms.

In the office, I was his number two, his right-hand man. Affectionately, people came to know me as his son. Adopted, of course, but still very much so his own kin. And he treated me this way. We worked together and I confided in him. After some time, I even moved into his mansion of a house. He had numerous bedrooms in his walk-up, allowing enough space for me to live quietly under his protection. He had numerous help to facilitate the upkeep; it was all dreamlike. From my rotting wooden house with dirt floors to a luxurious New York walk-up, I couldn't have dreamed a better scenario.

But brewing under the surface, the voices returned. Compelling and pandering me to act. I tried to quell them under the bottle, but that only worsened their heinous tone. Looking back, I could see myself falling apart. Piece by piece.

CHAPTER SIX

MY BODY LEAPT FROM THE bed, snatching the sheet to uncover what was beneath. Lying in bed, asleep, I woke to a slithering up my leg. The texture was warm and smooth, unusual and frightening. It started at my toes, following up my legs, moving sluggishly, making it difficult to discern my dream from reality. Initially, I panicked, watching the sheet rise to a silhouette figure with something slithering beneath. But a voice pulled me from my frozen state, prompting my legs to leap from the bed.

I pulled the sheet from the bed. Nothing.

For the first time in a long time, my body felt warm and energized. I felt a warmth running throughout my body. The pain had all but disappeared under the guise of the abrupt warmth. My heart pounded against my rib cage, but the bitter temperatures crept back in. My breathing became heavy blankets that hung in the air, prompting me to quickly jump back into bed, despite my reservations.

Laying down, still unnerved, I tried to focus on my breaths as a distraction. But each breath was shallow and visible with each exhale. The stinging cold reminded me of my frequent walks on the streets of New York in the dead of winter. This was my alone time, wandering the streets, sitting with my thoughts, and revisiting my past. I couldn't speak to anyone regarding what I had endured, but in walking, my mind would clear, feeling a temporary relief of healing. It was more helpful then the endless bottles I fell into.

Each walk was followed by a new kill. I wanted to stop. Maybe turn myself in, to seek help. But I couldn't. A piece of me didn't know how to control that dark side; it was always looming over the rest of me, forcing its way through. This wasn't who I wanted to be. But the voices were incessant. They never quelled until the act was done. The reprieve would be temporary, weeks even, until they started again.

The men Charles associated with were not good men. Already taking advantage of the law, they had other fetishes that needed to be satiated. And their openness to indulge was nauseating.

I remember one client, Alistair, a younger man, closer to my age, near thirties, preparing a large celebratory party for his recent industrial achievement. Charles and I attended, as he was a high-profile client with millions invested in Charles's business dealings. He paraded these young boys around, touching them and whispering in their ears. It pulled me back into the basement with Paul, chaining me to those thoughts. My discomfort was clear, scratching deep marks into Alistair's wooden table, locking onto him. The voices encircled, flashing Paul's image over Alistair.

Late that night, after the party was settled and the final guest had left, I hid in a closet, having told Charles I was heading to a lady friend's house. I watched him through the crack of the door, his drunken stupor gave me the edge I needed. His belt was useful in hanging him from his bedpost. The façade of suicide wouldn't be easy, but I managed to have him whip up a quick note pleading to his undesirable behavior before I killed him.

Watching his lifeless body hang from his bedpost, barely drifting side to side, I sat back in his leather chair in the corner of the room, a glass of bourbon in hand, looking to his bloodshot eyes. The voices were congratulatory and the bourbon slid down smoothly. The image of the basement never left me. The chains binding only tightened and the glass of bourbon turned into bottles.

But the evil didn't stop with him. He was the first as an adult. I had never considered killing again after Paul. I didn't even consider Paul as someone I killed. I fought back against him. Fought back against his cruelty and inhumanity. With Alistair, the rage flowed deep within my veins, quelled only by his lifeless body. The feeling was insatiable. But I made no plans to kill again. But there are different levels to evil, real evil. People fear the ghosts in stories and fables, but the real monsters are very much so alive and human.

My father was my introduction into the world of inhumanity. But my next encounter was far more sinister than I could have imagined, forever transforming me into the killer I am today.

I had dreamed for years of escaping the abuse inflicted by my father, but it all seemed a fairytale for me. Until Jim unexpectedly died. Too many drunken nights finally found their way through his system, destroying him from within. Not a tear was shed in my household. His passing provided the launching pad for both of us to live out the life we wanted, separate from each other.

I couldn't bare the stench of despair in that small town. Those who stayed were suffocated until every last breath was squeezed out, mercilessly. I needed a way out. I had nothing. If I stayed, I would've become nothing. The decision to leave was a foregone conclusion. I left a handwritten note on my pillow addressed to Clara and set forth on my journey. Taking my only other pair of clothes, age worn shoes, and a loaf of bread, I set out through the countryside to the Big Apple, with dreams and hopes guiding me.

It's easy to leave nothing in hopes of something, anything that's real and tangible. That's what gave me hope, and that's what kept me alive. That's what still keeps me alive.

New York was only a few hours' drive, but on foot, it would take much longer. Hitchhiking and stealing food would be the best manner of survival. I just needed to get there. The rest didn't matter. I had no plan. But I trusted things would work out.

I spent hours combing through the backwoods forests, running from snakes, and tending to my wounds inflicted from the branches and trees slicing against my arms. Ready to give up, I had come to an open road.

Enthusiastically walking alongside it, thankful to be out of the trees and bushes in the late hours, the sound of an engine coming from behind startled me. The truck slowed, approaching me.

"Hey kid, where ya headed?"

"New York City."

"Need a ride? I can get you there. It's not too far. I'm heading that way to see a friend anyway. Go ahead and jump on in!"

He seemed warm and friendly. His welcoming smile prompted me to enter his truck. Introducing himself as Paul, he cracked a few jokes, putting me at ease. We spoke about my journey and where I was headed. He even offered some helpful tips, buildings to remember, and streets to avoid. His soft voice was kind and sincere, a relief to the yelling I had become accustomed to.

In the middle of our conversation, intently locked into his life story, I felt a sudden and violent shift in the truck, pulling me heavily to one side. His smile morphed into a sinister scowl with his foot pressing deeply onto the accelerator. We were flying through some backwoods area, funnels of dirt flying through the air, rocks smacking against the windshield.

Coming to a secluded driveway at the end of a forested area, I could see a house coming into view. His foot stomped on the break, thrashing my head against the dashboard. Bits of sound creeped through, the keys turning and the car door opening before it all melted into a blur.

A scurrying sound startled me awake. My foggy eyes willed open, crusted from seemingly hours of having been shut. The room blurred around me, desperately blinking to restore my sight. A shadow figure moved in the distance shuffling through some items on a work bench.

Panicked, I motioned my hands to rub at my eyes but a force pulled me back. Attempting again, my arms felt heavy and immobile. I squeezed my eyelids tightly, forcing the tears to water through and clear my vision. Thankfully, it worked. But the sight wasn't anything to be thankful for. My arms were tightly bound to pieces of rope attached from one wall to the other. Sweat beads gathered and engulfed the back of my neck while a trembling settled deep within my bones.

I tried to pull against the rope, using my body weight, but it was knotted tightly in the secured metal loop. My strains were audible but unnoticeable to me until I heard the clank of a tool falling to the ground. The room fell silent. My heart beating harshly against my chest, I glanced over at the figure I had remembered.

His weighty breath filled the void of silence. His exhales were deep and prolonged. His shoulders grew with each breath, but his body remained, still, frozen, narrowing his blacked eyes on me. He cocked a left sided smile, revealing his cleft lip.

"My, my, my, awake now are we? Just in time for all the fun."

He lifted a gun held from behind him, pointing it at me.

"I *can* kill *you*."

His finger laid still on the trigger but he did not press. A warning.

A smirk arose on his malevolent face.

I couldn't move. I was frozen. I should've tried to pull on the rope harder. I should've fought back. But I didn't. I couldn't. Fear was no longer just a word. It was real. It was tangible.

He began to walk toward me as he unbuttoned his pants. All I could do was pull my knees to my chest, pressing my eyelids shut, tears cascading.

That night and many days, weeks that followed, he stole not only my innocence but a piece of my soul. A piece that has never returned. His actions were violent, ripping me in two. I couldn't decide which pain was worse, the emotional or physical toll. My body ached for a reprieve, even a day, but he never remitted. He took a sick pleasure in using me, my body. Lighting a cigarette after each encounter, he would stare at me, pleased with himself, ogling at my body, smiling.

Every ounce of faith I had in people was ruptured.

I had nearly lost faith in myself. I became weak. I blamed myself. Feeling ashamed. Getting lost deep within my head, my anxieties, my emotions. I felt I had let this happen, letting my guard down too early. I wasn't careful enough discerning him.

With every passing hour, every passing day of being tied in that basement, I tried to regain my will to live again. It slowly dissipated. I wanted to die.

A piece of me had come to expect his sickening urges; it was routine. But another piece, a darker piece was building. A wave threatening to fall. Rage, hatred, something more dangerous, more heinous than I could comprehend. It was taking me to a place I had yet to enter.

All excitement I felt for a new life blackened. A cloud of darkness fell upon me. My thoughts drifted away from appeasement to my next move: How I would kill him.

A smile was no longer welcomed on my face. Emotionally devoid.

Yet, he trusted me, even trying to befriend me. It was vile. I vomited violently after every interaction, waiting until he left up the steps, closing the door. Rocking myself in the corner, the desire to kill him grew. The voices started. The words were encouraging, assuring me he would fall. And I talked back with them, willfully, gleefully. My only friends.

Hatred was consuming me, from my limbs to my heart. I wanted him dead, I needed him dead.

Time dragged forward, each passing day came with new information. His name was really Paul, and he lived alone. He was the last of his name. His mother died upstairs a few months prior. He cried of his loneliness and the comfort I now offered. As his mouth moved, the voices rang louder, calling on me for action. But my body remained disciplined, biding my time. And the time came.

A loud banging on the door upstairs startled him, twisting his head up the staircase before turning his peering eyes back to me.

"Who could that be?"

My eyes never left his. Paul struggled to stand up, cautiously walking up the stairs. In his alarmed state, he dropped his work knife. It sat there pressed against the concrete, glistening toward me, awaiting my reach.

Quickly, I scrambled to grab it with my feet. After many unsuccessful attempts, my toes finally latched onto it, slicing at the inner skin but bringing it to my one free arm. I quickly buried it into the dirt behind me, knowing he would return.

Frantic, he sprinted down the stairs, nearly missing the bottom step. Paul scurried to me, lifting the gun to the middle of my face.

"If ya make one fucking noise I'll blow yer face right off, do you understand?"

I lifted my shoulders in agreement.

Satisfied, he scurried up the stairs, locking the door at the top.

He failed to tie my hand back up, leaving me with a free arm and a knife. My friends were ecstatic. *It's time.*

Shuffling and hollering penetrated through the floor above me. Then a final slam of the front door prompted Paul's return. This time, he held a dish with him, glee shining through him.

"Well, they won't be bothering us no more." He chuckled.

"Boy, you did good. Yes, ya did. Yer were quiet. Just like I asked. I brought you an extra treat. Here. Go on, try it."

He dropped to his knee, landing at eye level with me, pushing a piece of yellow cake up to my face in expectation. My eyes fell to it in disgust.

"Oh, come on now. It's not going to bite ya! Just grab it! It's good, I promise! Now come on, take a bite!" he insisted, annoyance in his tone.

Paul pushed it up to my face. I studied the piece intently; my eyes bouncing between his face and the cake. Each second that passed, his annoyance turned to anger. Not wanting to waste my chance, I popped the cake into my mouth. My eyes locked onto his, persevering through the dry, wretched sponge substance. My stomach churned in horror as the abomination slid down into my gut, but my eyes remained glued on him.

His laughter roared through the air, cocking his head back, then tilting his chin forward to me. His fat fingers lifted a large piece of cake into his hand, pushing it into his mouth. Paul began to reminisce about his mother and her excellent baking skills. My mind went elsewhere.

Paul put down the remaining cake and licked his fingers as his eyes ogled my body, looking me up and down before saying it was "time." He stood up to unbutton his pants, unholstering his overgrown belly. Bending down on each battered knee, he motioned to climb on top of me.

As his head slid down to bare a kiss on my neck, I snapped my head and drew out the knife plunging it into his oversized neck. The feeling was euphoric. The voices cheered in approval. Prompting me to continue. The blows were quick and deep, a red crimson splattering across the walls.

I felt alive again. My mouth dropped open as I watched the expression on his face quickly change. I soaked in his desperate pleas and agony, letting it wash over me. The wave had fallen, taking me with it.

The sensation was insatiable. Quickly, I pulled the sharpened tool out and I thrusted it continuously into his neck. Trails of blood whipped from the knife. His eyes widened to where they looked like they may pop out; he desperately clutched at his neck. His bewildered mouth fell open, emptying a red wave over my dirt ridden body.

His struggling ceased and his eyes fixed on the ceiling above.

I struggled to push him off, but after a few heaves, I was able to do so. I shook my arms and wiggled my fingers to crush the trembling of my hands. My blood stained hands cut my other arm loose, physically freeing my body.

I knelt down and watched the color drain from his lifeless body. The voices quelled. Only my heavy breathing was audible. I lifted my hands before my face noticing a deep smile cracking through. I couldn't remember the last time I smiled as I did.

Biting on my lower lip, I rose from the floor, grabbing a shop towel from the work bench and wiping my soiled face. Walking to the staircase, I sat down on the first stair, observing the sight. For the first time, I felt in control, powerful, and no longer a victim to circumstance. *This is what alive feels like.*

That memory faded into the dark abyss but left a stinging lingering blow. Standing from my bed in the asylum, I walked to my bowl of water. Cupping the water in my hands, I stared at my reflection, noticing a tear dropping into the bowl, creating ripples. I held the water in my hands, trying to compose my quaking self.

Sighing first, I forcefully exhaled, reopening my eyes, peering into the reflection.

My eyes open, jaw fell slack, eyebrows furred. The reflection gleaming back was not mine. The space of the room shallowed and the oxygen evaporated. I could not breathe, I could not think. The image bore its eyes into me, corrupting my thoughts. Its presence was clear. I was no longer alone in this room anymore.

CHAPTER SEVEN

DROPPING THE WATER, I STEADILY backed away, my mouth still open in disbelief. My left hand ran up my face into my hair. *What was that?*

Unsettling thoughts shifted in my head, wondering if what I had seen was real.

A biting wind smacked across my body, extracting the hair up from my arms, revealing the lining goosebumps. A shadow loomed over me, penetrating through the light, shielding me in darkness. My heart wasn't racing, in fact, it felt as if it was slowing down. As if I was ceasing to be. My shallow breaths were visible but my mind had to beckon my lungs to breathe. The darkness above encircled, delegating as a tornado of terror.

My toes dug into the ground below, wanting to remain stable and steady. The chattering of my teeth lifted my ears from the ringing. A swirl of voices twirled openly around me, luring me into the sounds. The voices were indiscernible, starting as an uneasy chorus of whispers. The room was swallowing me into this glacial hell. If I hadn't reached the ninth circle of hell, I knew I was close.

My rabid trembling exhausted me in ways I had not imagined. The icy temperatures pierced through my body, freezing me from the insides. My eyes were growing heavy while my lungs felt suffocated by a block of rising ice.

A hauntingly scornful scream broke through the iceberg building inside of me. The sound penetrated through my ears, viciously echoing in my mind. My hands flung to cup my ears, but the piercing noise wreaked havoc inside, reverberating longer, louder.

My mouth dropped to yell, but my sounds ran silent. The piercing noise trounced all audibility, desiring to be the only focus. Collapsing under the exhaustion of my body, my legs collapsed from beneath me. Straightaway, the sound vanished.

Able to breathe, I took a deep inhale trying to restore the oxygen to my head. But an unpleasant smell stunned my senses. The smell of burning human flesh was rife in the air. Its stench was heavy and thick, masking the usual decay of this room. But the overwhelming shrill powered through, carrying louder, as I had reached my overwhelming limit.

The dark fog vanished above me, allowing an obscure light through the crevice of my door.

I could hear panic and shouting outside in the hallway, but I could not discern what was being said. Everything sounded muffled, my ears recovering.

Sitting up from the wall, I shook my head awake. Trying to knock away the sudden onset drowsiness that had plagued me during the shrill, I palmed at my eyes furiously.

Is this a damn dream? This isn't real. It can't be.

Trying to stand felt as if I was lifting myself from ice. After several attempts, I slid down the wall in defeat. The screams and fiery of panicked yells outside my door drifted into focus.

"Help! Help! He's on fire! For God's sake, anyone! Help him! Now! Somebody! Help him!" The screams looped, repeating themselves in a voice I was unable to fully recognize.

No! No! You're dreaming! Wake up! This isn't real, damnit! Wake up!

My right hand quickly rose to my face, slapping myself repeatedly, hoping, praying this was a dream that I just needed to wake from. Every night, nightmares have plagued me, making it difficult to identify the real world or the dream one. The nightmares were cruel and malign, but I seemed to wake before the evil fully reached me, yet.

But why haven't I awoken yet? Why is this still happening? Wake up damnit!

I smacked my face one last time, drawing up as much energy as I could, but the blistering feeling echoed an alarming sentiment: *I am awake.*

My head fell back in disbelief.

How? If this is real then . . . Dear God.

The screams outside came back into focus. I needed to know what was going on out there. Pulling my legs to my chest, I made a feeble attempt to stand once more. My body felt heavier than I had remembered, and I felt frail, old, and tired.

What is wrong with me?

I just didn't have the strength to stand, but the putrid smell was horrid, churning my stomach violently. I couldn't help but to roll over and vomit on the floor next to me. It was overpowering all my senses. It felt so close. As if I was in the room itself. I could almost see the image. A man on fire, his flesh melting away from his body. Piece by piece dripping down like wax on a burning candle.

Smoke lingered under my door, littering my room with a gray fog, burning at my eyes. A coughing fit exploded out of my mouth, fatiguing me further. My chest ached for relief, but my eyes fell heavy, plunging back into my skull.

"Lyle! Lyle! Get your ass up boy! You're going to die in here if you keep smelling that shit! Get up!"

A violent jerking of my collar pulled me from my dream state, but my eyes would not open. I had lost all my energy.

"Stupid shit! Lucky I pulled you out of there! Could've died in there, ya know? Should've let you, one less psycho walk—"

"Shh. Shh. Now, now, Richard. We don't have to go around talking this way. No, no. We don't speak like that in front of—Mr. Lockehart's death was . . . simply an accident. It's an old building, these things happen. You should know this. And he wasn't in his right mind. Now, splash some water on Mr. Lyle's face and get him cleaned up. He smells as if *he himself* was in that damn fire. Get to it!" Dr. Holmes barked.

What did he just say? Dead? Fire? Christ . . .

A image was cast upon me, whipping my head back. I could see him. Lockehart shrieking in agony, helpless as the fire around consumed him, melting his flesh, cooking him internally. Even on fire, his fists thrusted against the door, pleading for someone to let him out.

The sight dissolved, returning me to my own thoughts.

Christ, is any of this real?

"Here! Here's a towel, wipe your damn face." Dick shouted as he threw a damp towel in my face.

The smoke's wrath must have been visible on my face. The coolness of the towel was a welcome to my burning eyes. I wiped my face finally, regaining my full vision.

I only recognized Tommy. I could see him rolling his wheelchair to make his way to me.

"Lyle, are *you* alright? We—I thought that was *you* screaming? It sounded just like you!" Tommy whispered in concern.

"What the hell is going on here, Tommy? Was that Lockehart I heard? Was he on fire?"

"I do—I dunno. This, all of it, I can't seem to understand any of it."

"Well, frankly, I don't know what the fuck is going on. What is real, what isn't? I feel like I'm losing my Goddamn mind here, Tommy. So please, if you can, help me out here. Please?"

I was desperate. Tommy could see this. But his face reflected a noticeable discomfort. He looked scarred, frozen in his horror.

"It just—I dunno. Really. I was being pushed to my room by Dick when he noticed Lockehart's door was cracked open. He stopped. We were both unnerved by it. You know how thick these damn doors are. They don't just open by themselves. That asshole screamed at me not to move. Me? Me! In a fucking chair!"

"Yes, Tommy, I get that, continue, please."

"Well, he threw open the door and we both could see it. Could see him. He was just standing there, based in the dark. The room reeked of turpentine. How the fuck he managed that? I dunno. But it smelt like the whole damn place would blow."

"He was alive when you saw him?"

"Scary, huh? He's the one who lit the match, right in front of us. I could see the outline of his face. He was smiling, Lyle! That psycho was smiling. It was—it was fucking evil. He just dropped the match on the floor like it was nothing. The flames, they were everywhere! He didn't even fucking scream. He just stood there!"

"He didn't scream? He didn't try to leave? Are you sure?"

"Yes, yes! I could never forget a sight like that! It's fucking burned into my memory, quite literally."

"This . . . this doesn't make any sense . . ."

"Nothing here does . . . Nothing ever will."

"Did anyone try to help him?"

"Who? Dick? Fuckin' coward. When the flames got too big, he shut the door on him. Trapping him in there! I rolled toward Dick, kicking and trying to pull him off, but I couldn't. But then the screams came . . ."

"I thought you said he didn't scream?"

"No, Lyle. *You* did. They came from *your* room!"

My lips were left without words. I sat back, aghast.

"You sounded, you sounded as if you were on fire. I thought you were dying! I screamed for help, calling for someone to check on you. Finally, Dr. Holmes came and made Dick go in there to fetch you. I can't, I can't even explain it. Not even dear ole Doc there could. They just pulled you out, refusing to answer my questions. I thought you were dead. This fucking place. It's evil, all of it. I can't—"

"Tommy! Tommy, calm down. You're not right. It couldn't have happened that way. I *saw* the smoke penetrate under my door after the screaming initiated. Lockehart couldn't have been locked in there! I saw the fucking smoke with my own two eyes! You're crazy. You really are fucking insane!"

"No, dammit! Listen to me, Lyle!"

I could tell he was frightened. He reached down and pulled me up to his level by my collar. His eyes had glossed over. The usually rosy cheeks were flushed out with white. I've never seen a man as terrified as Tommy was. His grip on my collar tightened.

"There is something wrong with this place. I see, I see these shadows at night. They lurk in my nightmares. I hear wailing and screaming. I've even been woken up to this, this thing standing above my bed. It was, it was just there. It didn't have a face but I knew it was staring at me. I just knew it. I could feel it wants me dead. It's not going to stop, Lyle. It *needs* me to suffer. It has been visiting me every night. I can't sleep, I can't eat. It's always lurking, it's always there. It's not even fucking human. I can feel it, I know it. I can *still* feel it."

Tommy was damn near about to burst into tears. I've never seen a man so frazzled, so unnerved.

"Don't look at me like the loon here, Lyle. I hear you, too. Before *that* thing started to haunt me, I could hear you, begging, pleading in your sleep. It isn't just me. This place has been placated by strange happenings. Fifty-two patients have committed suicide here. Fifty-Two! This damn place should be shut down and burned to a proper fucking crisp if Dr. Satan-Incarnate over there wasn't bribing state officials. Keep tightly to your head! I'm warning you."

His warning lingered with me, reverberating deep within my soul. He was right. I have seen and felt something odd here. I never believed in God, demons, angels, or anything spiritual. I always believed that to be hokey. I mean, in my life, if there was a God, where was he? Where was he when I was getting beaten by my father? Where was he when I was locked in that fucking basement? Through all the fucking betrayals? Where was he?

But I don't know if it's madness setting in or if there is something to this place, but I haven't felt the same since I stepped foot into this hell.

Tommy was just opening his mouth to speak when Dr. Holmes walked in.

CHAPTER EIGHT

"GENTLEMEN! GENTLEMEN. EVERYTHING IS FINE and we can now return to our rooms and routine. There shall be no more disturbances for the night. Prepare for the morning's festivities!" Dr. Holmes stated with a obsequious tone.

There was something so unusually off about Dr. Holmes's demeanor. For a man to burn to death while under his care, he seemed rather put together. He always did. His composed manner was what unnerved me most about him.

Out of all the men confined to this asylum Tommy has regaled me with, Dr. Holmes still frightens me the most. His comfortableness with morbidity, with death, is far beyond even myself, someone who has seen his fair share of dead men.

Tommy seemed to know a great deal about the men caged here. Unfortunately for him, he has been here for years, biding his time, waiting for any chance to return to a "normal" life. Locked in here, I no longer believe "normal" to exist. It lives as a fairytale to everyday people, calming their nerves and cloaking them from the oddities of the word.

"I've had quite the lot of roommates before you, Lyle. But you are the one who's most "normal.""

"Christ, you *must* have met some psycho's in your time."

Tommy and I enjoyed a chuckle.

"You can only imagine."

"Try me."

Tommy's first roommate was a body with multiple men trapped inside.

"Barnes, well the nice side of him was called this. He ran a few different Juice Joints. He peddled with a few big-timers back in New York and all across the coast. But if you crossed him, Lorne would make his presence known."

I sat and listened to Tommy explain how Lorne would carve out the eyes and tongues of all those who were caught squealing to the cops about his personal dealings. Law enforcement had a hard time making a case because each witness would end up recanting or get bumped off. It was genius really. He had this going all through the '20s. But one simple slip up of loose lips with an undercover copper got him pinched and a raid on his house. The dumb sap had a collection of eyeballs and tongues in mason jars in his living room above his fireplace. He was sent here while awaiting trial but deemed even too crazy even for prison.

"He was a poor roommate. Bickering between his selves throughout the night. I managed a few conversations with him, but then the screaming began. It was insufferable. Scratching sounds followed. They had to confine him to this jacket to stop him. Damn near filed down his fingernails. Dr. Holmes took him from his room—well, now, *your* room—and I never heard about him again. Rather unlucky, I say."

"What is?"

"Your room. Well, now. *You.*"

"Why's that?"

"Not one has lasted as long as you have. Well, without going mad."

"Gentlemen, to your rooms, now. Follow please."

Dr. Holmes and Dick escorted us back to our rooms. Tommy and I had a long stare between us. I had this dark feeling deep within that this may be the last time I see Tommy. I think he felt it too.

The door slammed shut and the lock clicked.

Christ!

My heart leapt out of my chest and down my throat. I stammered back leaning heavily on the wall behind me. I could feel the crinkle of my forehead as my eyebrows lifted in fear.

Opposite me, situated in the corner, stood a silhouette of a figure. Through the faintness of light from the hallway combing through, I could see an outline. I could not make out a face, nor any recognizable features. My eyes scanned what I could see, but either in terror or in protection, a full image would not capture. Blinking my eyes furiously, I tried to blink away the sight. But it remained, motionless and isolated.

My heavy breathing and beating heart added to a rising temperature building in the room. A blistering heat wave danced across my body, pulling the sweat from my pores.

My eyes motioned to the door, wondering if I could escape or call for help. I cocked my head to the door but noticed the light was receding from my room. Darkness was overtaking the area.

No, no, no, no. Fuck! Fuck! Fuck!

I needed to scream but my mouth wouldn't move. My senses were frozen, out of my control. My eyes returned to search for the figure. But my heart nearly sank to the floor. It was drifting closer, hunched over as it moved. Nearly within reach.

I opened my mouth to yell but nothing came out.

My heart began to make leaps out of my chest. It was beating so hard I feared it would burst. Fear or whatever *It* was had engulfed me.

It was there. Here. Inches from me. *It's* presence was unnerving, gut-wrenching. Churns spurred around in my stomach, my body rejecting this moment. Vomit rose up from my stomach and into my mouth, sitting there, too terrified to spew. The fear pressed tightly into my bladder, forcing me to stand in a puddle of my own discomfort.

My mind was trying to conceptualize what I was looking at but it just couldn't. As I was staring at this creature, I couldn't explain what I was seeing. A fog reached into my mind, clouding over. *Its* image too frightening to leave as a memory. It wasn't human. It wanted to be. But it just wasn't. I have read countless scary stories of creatures and demonic monsters with red eyes and fangs for teeth, but this entity wasn't of that mold.

The longer I stared, the more I tried to picture, to make out anything of this entity. It looked, it looked almost like me. A caricature of what I looked like, staring back at me. It was as if I was looking into a sinister fun house mirror. I felt a drop stream down my face from the corner of my eye. But it wasn't a tear. A drop of blood streamed from my eyes, a burning sensation following. The blood vessels in my eyes tightened, my head squeezing together, feeling as though my head was caught in between a crank, tightening more and more. The entity moved in closer, entrapping me between *IT* and the wall. There was nowhere to go, nowhere to run. The air was being sucked out of the room, my lungs collapsing in this condensed moment. The entity's breath was felt on my cheeks, causing me to turn my head away, eyes squeezing shut. A tang of gin whiffed heavy in the air, clouding my sense of smell. My drink of choice after every kill, this was a heinous mockery.

The entity moved in even closer, pressing me up against the wall, within a breath from my face. I felt a cold brush of a finger slide up from my neck to my jaw. I clenched my teeth, trying not to make a sound, my fingernails digging into the wall. I kept my eyes locked tightly shut; what was to come, I did not want to see. The finger slid upward again, moving to my left temple, pressing deeply inward, pushing my head against the wall.

An image flashed into my mind. I was on my hands and my knees, begging upward, pleading as tears streamed down my face. A gun pressed up into my left temple, the shooter caught beneath a drifting fog.

I watched as the shooter pulled back the trigger and then the room fell dark.

"What's this? Look at ya! Laying in y'er own piss now, are ya? Get yourself together! Ya overslept for y'er appointment with Dr. Holmes! Get cleaned up, now, get to it! We haven't all day!"

Dick threw a wet rag in my face, frightening me awake. My eyes shot open to see the creature hanging from the wall, just above my bed, peering down at me.

CHAPTER NINE

I DARED NOT MOVE. I wasn't even sure if I was fully awake. Could I still be partially dreaming? Was it even a dream? What I see looks awfully real to me. Hidden only in the darkness of the corner to others, I knew *IT* was there. I was too afraid to move, too afraid to even take my eyes from what I was seeing.

"I asked ya to get ready, now didn't I?" Dick bellowed, pulling my arm, lifting me from my bed.

But my head remained tilted upward, staring.

"Now you listen to me ya crazy shit! Ya smell like hell and I can't let you leave like this, not in front of *him*. Now you get ready right now or I'll strip ya down myself!"

Dick pulled my shirt, lifting it above my head. I panicked, feeling confined and encroached upon. My arms flailed, trying to take the shirt from my head.

"Let me help ya, you fool! Crazy bastard! Whaddya looking at anyway, huh?"

Dick's eyes examined the ceiling.

But it was gone. Twisting my head, I searched all around, looking for the entity. But it had vanished.

"Y'er getting crazier and crazier by the minute! Here, take these clothes right here. Put 'em on, hurry up!"

Dick pushed some garments into my arms, but I still remained hesitant. But Dick's hefty push nearly sent me on my back, pulling me from fear and into anger.

"Well move it, now, will ya?"

I removed my soiled clothes then entered into the new ones, glaring at Dick the entire time. Once I had finished dressing, I walked up, meeting him face-to-face. My fists balled, jaw clenched, shoulders rising. But Tommy's voice echoed in my mind, dissuading me from acting upon my frustration.

"Lyle, ya can't let him get you all riled up like that. He's an asshole! Don't give him the satisfaction. They want you to act. They want you to be that violent psycho y'er painted as. But that's not you. Fight it! You can do it, I know you."

"Do you, Tommy?"

"You're better than you think you are, Lyle. Don't let them kill you. You already do enough of that yourself."

I dropped my balled fists and loosened my stance.

"After you, of course." Dick sneered at me before waving me forward.

I glanced one last time up in the corner of the ceiling, relieved to still see nothing. I cocked my head back at Dick before taking a step to exit the room. I nearly breathed a sigh of relief, thankful to be exiting this room.

I must be losing my damn mind in here.

Stepping into the hall, my shoulders lifted, taking a deep inhale, thankful to be anywhere but in *there*. The confinement is playing tricks on me, I was sure of it. But a different type of hell awaits.

I turned back around to see if Dick was following but stumbled backward.

"Tommy?"

Tommy's face startled me, fixing me in place.

What in the hell is this?

My head lifted, bewildered, horrified. Dick was gone. I wasn't even in the hallway anymore. Bookshelves lined all around me. Thousands of books in my peripheral. I was situated in the library. Tommy was sitting at a table flipping through his books.

"Well, it's about damn time, Lyle! Had me waiting for quite the lot, now didn't ya?" Tommy pointed to his wrist, motioning a fake watch.

I said nothing, eyes lining the room, the oxygen barely returning to my lungs.

"Ya look like you've seen a ghost! You alright?" Tommy questioned, concerned.

"Here, just have a seat, Lyle. Come on, now. Sit right here." Tommy motioned for me to sit. But I was leery, skeptical if this was even real.

"Come on, sit, Lyle. You're freaking me out, now." Tommy's eyes widened, even he was leery.

My feet finally moved, unglued from the floor. Taking small steps, I studied all of which was around me. This *was* the library. I had been here many times before with Tommy. Before, before I was thrown into full confinement. Some of my favorite memories are pictured here, reading novels and different stories with Tommy, making light of our pasts and speaking of a future that, deep down, knew we would never enjoy.

I reached for the wooden chair, pulling it backward, still disoriented, baffled at this all.

"Well, it took ya long enough! Right, I picked out this one, whaddya think? I read the ending, sounds like a good book to me!"

Tommy always had a habit of reading the endings. He never liked reading a book with a bad ending. He said we lived in a world of bad already, we didn't need to add to it with fictional stories of the same.

"Lyle, are you listening to me? What do you think of this one?"

He pushed the book up to me, beckoning for me to give it a chance.

My mind scrambled to put together words, trying to string along a sentence. At that moment, I forgot how to speak. Unable to utter a word, I nodded in approval, hoping this would be enough for now.

"Hmph, I think you'll like it. It has to be better than the book we read last week, anything would be better than that travesty!"

Tommy chuckled, looking to me to laugh with him. I half-heartedly smiled up at him, my nerves still shot from the preceding events. He sensed something was off, leaning in to whisper.

"Is everything alright, mate? You seem . . . well, off."

I buried my hands in my face, only able to utter, "I don't know."

"Well, you better snap out of it, ya have an appointment today with Dear ole Doc, now don't ya?"

My hands dropped from my face.

How did he know? My God, what is happening?

"Relax, mate. You told me last night." His brow furrowed, giving me an uneasy stare.

"Something's off."

"You don't say?" Tommy laughed.

"No, Tommy, something is really wrong. I can't explain it. You'll think I was mad. But something is really wrong here, I just . . ."

My words halted as my eyes wondered to the corner of the room. The entity had returned. Waving at me with a distorted smile.

"Ayo, mate!" Tommy snapped his fingers in my face, breaking my gaze. "You're not really going mad now, are ya?"

"Huh?" My eyes returned to Tommy. "I'm sorry, I haven't slept much lately. I keep having these, these dreams. Nightmares really. This place must be getting to me." I tried to smirk, but my eyes returned to the corner: the entity had vanished.

Tommy cocked his head back, looking in the same direction.

"Ya know, Lyle, y'er starting to scare me. I heard you last night. Screaming. You kept on for some time. But that's not the worst of it. I heard voices. Like you were talking to someone. And something was talking back. It was real hushed, couldn't understand a thing you were saying, but you sure had me scared stiff."

Tommy's words fell to a distant echo while my eyes searched the room swiftly, looking for the entity.

"Lyle!" Tommy pounded his fist against the table. "Y'er starting to look as crazy as they make you out to be!"

The bang against the wooden table startled me, sending me back into my chair.

Drooping down in the chair, I tried to compose myself.

"Look, I'm sorry, Tommy. I don't know what's going on right now. I really don't. I feel like I'm losing sight of reality. Things keep on changing. Rapidly too. You wouldn't understand. Hell, I don't even either."

The grandfather clock at the end of the room struck 3:00 p.m., chiming at an unusually loud volume.

"Is the clock always this loud?" I placed my hands over my ears, wanting to drown out the sound.

"Why are you yelling? And what sound? What clock?"

"That one, that one right there!" I pointed to the grandfather clock, the chime intensifying its tone.

"Where? I'm not seeing what you are pointing at."

"Right—"

I stood up in disbelief. There was no clock. There was no chime.

"What in the hell? I swear, Tommy, I swear it was just there!"

"I'm starting to really worry about you, Lyle. . ."

I dropped back into the chair, my palms wiping at my eyes.

Christ. I'm falling apart here. Get it together man!

I lifted my head to speak to Tommy but nearly fell out of my chair. The entity was towering just above Tommy, peering down at him, that distorted menacing smile etched deeply into its face.

My stomach twisted in deep knots. My body harshly trembled, frozen in fear.

The entity turned its dead, cold blue eyes toward me, lifting its finger to its mouth. It hushed me before snapping its finger.

"Help! Lyle! What is this? Why are we here?" Tommy cried out, wading on a patch of broken ice.

"I don't know Tommy! I don't know what's going on!" I cried in bewilderment.

How could this be?

I looked down and could see myself on a separate patch of ice floating in the bluest of oceans. I stood in a frozen veneer. We were surrounded by miles of ocean in a frozen mountainside. The initial dusting of snow turned into fierce and treacherous blankets of heavy falling white, compromising my vision.

"Tommy! Tommy! Can you hear me? This storm is picking up. I need to know you are still near!"

"Lyle, I can't see a thing. The damn snow is blinding. You sound close! Can you get to me?"

"I don't know. I can't see myself!"

Bending down, I pressed against the ice, feeling the firmness before I attempted any such rescue.

It's firm. Maybe I can paddle to him?

As I reached for the water, my body tightened, a shadow deep within the water lurked beneath like a shark biding its time before striking. But I could hear Tommy frantically panicking in the distance. Gritting my teeth, I bent to reach my right hand into the water but immediately yanked it out, yelping in pain.

"What is it Lyle? What happened?" Tommy squalled.

"Fuck! This Goddamn water!"

"What? Is it too cold? What's going on?"

"No! It's too fucking hot! It's damn near boiling!"

My scorched fingers throbbed in pain, feeling as if I had placed my hand in a pot of hot soup.

"What . . . what do you mean it's hot? It's water Lyle! It's fucking snowing!"

"I don't fucking know, Tommy! Christ! We're stuck in the middle of a fucking blizzard! Nothing makes sense right now! Fuck!"

I dropped my hand into a hill of snow piled from the storm falling from above.

"Tommy, are you alright over there?"

My hand was falling numb in the snow, a better alternative to the scorched hell from moments before.

"Jesus, Lyle, do I seem alright? I'm floating on a fucking piece of ice! This. This cannot be real. No, no! This is not real!"

"Do you feel that frigid cold, Tommy? Can you feel the shivers running down your spine right now? Can you see the blue of the ocean surrounding us? Feel the wheelchair below you. Is it frozen? How much more fucking real does it have to get for you?"

Tommy stood quiet. Then a silence fell upon us. It was a feeling of melancholy that rained ever so slightly with the falling snow.

A sound bellowed in the distance striking a dagger of fear in my heart. I turned toward the sound and felt a wave of heat blitz across my face.

"Tommy! I can't see! Are you still there? I can't hear you!"

But a silence ensued. A deep and painful silence rang through.

I frantically tried to clear my eyes, aggressively rubbing against them with my hands, hoping to break free from the blindness that had so violently gripped me.

"Tommy! Can you hear me?" I barked, hoping for a sound, anything from Tommy.

Why isn't he saying anything?

I grabbed heaps of snow and tried to wash my eyes with it, needing to see, if only just a little. I rubbed some more getting a better visual. Tommy was mouthing something. But I couldn't make it out. It was quiet, eerily quiet. I squinted my eyes.

Is he? Is he screaming?

It looked as if Tommy was screaming for me, but no sound was emanating from his mouth.

"Tommy! I can't hear you! Can you hear me? Tommy! Wave your hands if you can hear me!"

I squinted again to see if he would respond. As I was looking, a piercing scream shot through my ears, penetrating my body. My body dropped down into the snow, my hands cupped over my distressed ears. The piercing bellowed in a more succinct and laborious tone.

The pain of the high-pitched scream felt as if it was going to blow out my ear drums. My stomach churned violently, causing me to turn on my side and vomit.

My body was fading in and out, and the ocean drifted from my eyes. As my eyelids grew heavy, the visual of Tommy descended further away. My body could take no more, and I drifted into the sea of darkness.

CHAPTER TEN

I AWOKE TO SNAPPING OF fingers and the visual of the entity fresh in my mind. Panicked, I jolted to my feet.

"Woah, woah, Lyle. Calm down. It's just me. It's Tommy. You fell asleep. Guess I was wrong about that book, aye?"

My heart nearly leapt out of my chest, calming down at the sight of Tommy's face.

"Christ, Tommy. You nearly scared me have to death." I dropped to place my hands on my knees, needing to catch my breath.

"Sorry! Sit. Unwind. Well, looks like I'm heading to see Dr. Holmes today, not you. Dick came in about fifteen minutes or so and informed me."

"Fifteen minutes? Was I out for that long?" I leerily sat down, perplexed at Tommy's words.

"Longer than that mate! But you seemed exhausted and needing of the rest. Those bags are really taking away your good looks! Better take more naps while you can." Tommy giggled.

"I am exhausted. You're right. All this not sleeping has me on edge. I just need a good sleep."

"Right you are!"

"So you are seeing Dr. Madman today, huh? Excited?"

"Hell no! That lunatic held me in an ice bath last time! Damn near froze to death! I can still feel, you know?"

The dream, the dream must have been a blending of what I remembered of Tommy's last meeting with Dr. Holmes and my sleep deprived mind. Thankfully, this seemed to put me at ease. Maybe the entity itself is but a figment of my restless mind.

"Did he say what you were doing today?"

"Jesus, the sick and twisted contraptions he comes up with never cease to amaze me. I truly believe he is trying to drive us mad. The whole lot of us. Well, if we weren't before. Between you and me, what did you call him?"

"Who? Dr. Holmes?"

"Yes."

"Oh, Dr. Madman?"

"Yes, as accurate a name as he deserves. His *treatments* are nothing but human torture experiments. Him, Dr. Price, all of them are nothing but sick sadists getting their jollies off to good ole fashioned human torture."

"Dr. Price? As in Price Institute?"

"Yes. Dr. V. Price. He was the founder here. Started it up in the late 1800s. Controversial place, even from the go. Ralph mentioned his father's corrupt dealings and this place was one of them. Hush money. Politicians campaigns get financing, and this place keeps their public funding. Torture, experiments, all of it free to continue. A few activists have been trying to get this place closed down, but they got the politicians by the balls. Money talks and owns."

"Where is Dr. Price?"

"Who knows? He disappeared a few years back."

"Disappeared? What does that even mean?"

"Who knows? They never found a body. He just vanished one day. No note, nothing. I think Dr. Madman, as you like to say, offed him. Sick bastard. Probably wanted full control. Who knows? Wouldn't put it past him to kill someone."

I opened my mouth to speak when Dick walked in, calling for Tommy to attend his appointment. Tommy flashed an uneasy attempt at a smile and rolled his wheelchair toward Dick. Tommy motioned to look back one more time, but Dick walked behind his chair to push him out of the room.

As I was about to stand up to leave the library, that familiar, horrific scream pierced my ears once again. It dropped me to my knees. The sound stifled any thought that had proceeded in my mind. I could feel the warm tears cascading down my face and the blow of nausea creep back into my lower stomach.

My eyes drew heavy, my consciousness fading between flickers of my heavy eyelids. Eyes closed, a cold wind caressed my face while the sound dissipated into silence.

My mangled mind slowly drifted back to reality, the biting wind making its unwelcome presence known. I couldn't even discern where the wind could have come from, too exhausted to care.

Under my arms, I felt cold hands hoist me from the floor. Attempting to lift my eyelids, I was immediately blinded by white lights hanging above, gleaming in my face.

My vision was still a blur but shadows of multiple figures surrounded me. Indistinct noises faintly made their way to my ears.

My legs could not support the weight bearing down on them, collapsing into whatever or whomever was holding me. The figure dragged my lifeless body across a cold cement floor. My left foot dragged particularly hard across, causing a sore on the outer area that riled me with some sense of striking pain.

I looked up to see the lights bearing down on me. As blinding as they were, it was comforting to know I wasn't in the darkness. The lights reached down to wrap me in its warm embrace, protecting me from what lingered in the dark. I reached out, hoping to meet its embrace, but my head snapped back, pushed into frigid waters.

My eyes shot open, horrified at the sight of the familiar waters. My only reprieve fell to the feeling of frigidity and not scorching temperatures as before. But the relief quickly dispersed. My body felt as if ice daggers were attacking in every direction. The icy waters were overwhelming, and I was deeply engrossed in it, drowning in its depths.

My teeth chattered and my heartbeat calmed to an unnaturally measured pace, having me question if I was alive or dead. I felt a sense of lightheadedness, and all I could see was an overwhelming hue of blue.

As the blue of the waters dissipated into an eternal blackness, a protruding angle of light danced gently across my face. With the remaining strength I had left, I forced my eyes open to survey what I could but to no avail. Drifting further into the depths of this ocean, my lungs felt ready to burst with the heaps of water streaming inward. I tried to paddle my arms to swim upward. I felt a sense of hope, but my lungs were screaming for relief, nearing cessation.

A light from what looked like the surface gave me that extra push to keep going, the will to live. I reached out to the light, feeling my finger escape the confinement of the water and breakthrough into air, but a burning sensation arose on my left forearm, pulling my arm back into the water. Floundering around, the stinging proliferated as I sucked in endless amounts of water, shrieking in pain. My eyes compacted and the world around me softened to a darkness.

"Mr. Lyle, you are back with us! Great news! You really shouldn't fall asleep in water. You could drown, you know? It's quite dangerous." Dr. Holmes sneered pulling my head up from the water.

Erupting into a coughing fit, my eyes squinted open, trying to assess who laid near. But the coughing consumed my body, causing Dr. Holmes to turn me on my left side as I vomited loads of water and some blood. My lungs thirsted for air, struggling to take in as much as it desperately required. My heart leaped in sporadic beats, thankful it had another chance to beat once more.

"You really should be much more careful, Mr. Lyle. What's this?"

Dr. Holmes bent to one knee, peering at my left arm.

"That's quite the nasty cut you have there. That looks quite serious. Yes, serious, indeed. How'd you manage that?"

He raised his eyes to mine, stone-faced while my coughing fit raged on.

"Well, we better patch you up immediately. Never know with curious injuries such as these . . . Richard, help him up before he bleeds all over my floor. Hurry up!"

Dick slowly wandered to me, lifting me forcibly up by my underarms, dragging me to another room. But even through the coughing fit, my eyes remained locked on my left forearm. The blood oozing out painted a stark picture. Certainty is an absolute illusion. The impossible has begun.

CHAPTER ELEVEN

I WOKE UP IN MY room after what felt like days later. My left arm had been bandaged, but the cloth had not been changed in some time, causing a minor stinging pain to my arm. I rubbed at my crusted eyes, lost to time and reality.

"Tommy?" I garbled, mouth painfully dry.

No answer.

"Tommy? Are you there? How long have I been out?"

Silence.

Angry growls of hunger panged at my stomach.

"Tommy!" I yelled one last time maneuvering my body to sit up.

Met with a spinning room, I dropped my arms to catch and center myself. I shook loose of the dizziness and proceeded to drop my legs to the cold concrete floor. I tried to stand but was met with opposition from my faint body. Hunger pains burned another round of scorn into my stomach, motivating me to try again, this time with more vigor. I finally stood and walked toward the metallic door. The hunger pangs roaring fiercely.

How long was I out? And where the hell is Tommy?

"Dick! Dr. Holmes! Hello? Anyone there?"

My fists pounded against the door, echoing throughout my room.

But no one came.

My calls bellowed into roars while I angrily kicked and pounded against the door. I was on the border of desperate and starving, a lethal combination. Desperation makes monsters of men. With each kick at the door, I could see the loss of muscle tone that had blended into a bone-skeleton look. I was not myself. I kicked and punched wrathfully but tiresomely. My body gave way and I collapsed with my legs underneath me, shrieking in pain before my head snapped against the flooring, sending a wave of black before me.

"Mr. Lyle. Mr. Lyle, can you hear me? Hello? Open your eyes, please?"

I groggily awoke to Dr. Holmes tapping on my forehead.

"Good. Good. You are back with us again. You seem to disappear quite often lately. Very curious creature you are. Indeed. It seems to me that you are passing through a rather difficult moment in your life. Perhaps, something is maligning your inner thoughts? Your mind? Your brain? I realize I have been quite lax with our treatments. As you know, we have many patients here at Price State Institute that I all, *personally*, attend to, requiring a near unmanageable schedule. But alas, here I am."

He shrugged near congratulatory.

"My apologies. But not to fear, my dear. For I am ready to help you embark on your next steps into a more comprehensive treatment. From the looks of it, you certainly require it."

I looked at my arms and my legs, spread, bound to chains pulling from the floor and the ceiling. I was suspended in the air held up by this chamber of sorts. My naked body poised in humiliation for all to see. The pulling of the chains was a discomfort I had never experienced. The chain was digging into my heels and wrists. The hunger that had once plagued my mind maligned into pure affliction.

My bones felt a pulling sensation at each crevice, as if he was ready to pull me apart, limb from limb. My trembling knees fell weak, but the unforgiving pull of the chains only tightened, stretching my body further. My heart galloped in my chest. Profuse streams of sweat lined my body, falling from my head to my toes.

"What is this? Why am I on this? What in the hell is going on here? Get me out of this now!"

My balled fists pulled against the chains hoping to break free, but the force repelled back, sinking me deeper into the contraption.

"What is this?" Dr. Holmes mocked. "Calm yourself, Mr. Lyle. This is not hell. This is the plan for your escape. Your mind, your body, locked in rigidity. This may seem unpleasant, presently, yes, yes it will. Quite. Naturally, look at what you are in. But you *need* this. A stretch of your imagination, so to speak, and your body." He sinisterly laughed.

"You son of a bitch!" I tried to reach out to him, but the chains whipped me back.

"Ah, yes. You are quite the candidate for this treatment. Stretching helps to improve the blood flow, to realign one with the body. I believe it to help with the mind as well. Discomfort and pain are not your enemies. Quite the contrary, my dear. They are friends of wisdom, molding and developing the *new* you! The new James Lee Lyle!"

"Go to hell!"

"Tisk, tisk." Dr. Holmes waved his finger near my face.

"Language like that will need to be quelled as well. Not to worry, that'll be another treatment down the road. Are you familiar with the term *lobotomy*? No? You will be soon!"

I blistered the air with oaths in protest. If I could have reached out to kill him, I would've squeezed every fucking drop of air out of his scrawny neck.

"Now, let's begin! Do get comfortable in your discomfort, you may be here for some time, Mr. Lyle. It's best to just let the journey lead you."

He pressed his hands together in glee as he walked out of the room. The door was shut and locked from the outside. The lights blared on, beaming down while the chamber's engine ignited.

A subtle circular motion commenced, bolstering as the time dragged on. I was unsure if I was spinning or if the room was. The menacing feeling of nausea returned with each increase of the turns. I was spinning at such a rate my eyes couldn't keep up.

Then everything stopped and it became clear. The entity emerged out of the darkness and maneuvered toward me. Through the spinning, *it* was all I could see. I focused intently to ease my worrying stomach and eyes. Oddly, he was a welcoming sight in the spinning chaos, giving me a tangible sight to focus on, to dispel the abrupt motion sickness plaguing my stomach. As I focused more intently, his callous blue eyes burned into mine. His grainy hand reached to my right cheek, calming the spinning of the room but drifting me into a world of darkness, *its* world. My head whipped back and my eyes closed.

CHAPTER TWELVE

"HEY THERE, BOY, ARE YOU alright?"

My eyes opened, and I was back in New York. I looked down and could see my disheveled, moth eaten clothes and the leftover food in my lap someone had thrown away days earlier.

"Say now, are you alright? Ya in this alleyway all by yourself?" The voice questioned insistently.

Sun beaming down into my eyes, I lifted my fingers to see the man standing above me. A whiff of that all too familiar musky cologne stiffened my body.

"Listen, kid, I'm Wyatt Halver. I own some of the rails around here and part of the country." He laughed. "Say, what's your name?"

My mouth dropped open, I couldn't believe who I was seeing.

How am I here? Again?

"Quiet type, huh? Say, how old are you, boy? You don't look much older than fifteen."

From the corner of my eye, I could see a black fog washing through. Wyatt began to disappear into the dark as his apartment appeared in sight.

"Lyle, take a seat please."

Wyatt emerged in front of me standing above his desk. My legs were already in motion, walking toward the seat he was motioning me to. As I sat down, he walked from behind his desk to the chair next to me.

"Now I've been good to you, right? I housed you, clothed you, the whole lot. Only a few weeks ago you were eating out of a trash can. Now, you're here. And you've caught on pretty quickly. But . . . I need something *more* from you. I need to *know* you really understand what you mean to *me* and I need to know how thankful you are. Are you following me, Lyle?"

I pleaded with my legs to get up and run, but they stood immobile. This memory wanted to play out. And I was afraid of *how much* it wanted me to relive.

"Lyle, follow please," Wyatt said, as he loosened his tie and walked toward the bedroom door.

"Now, boy!" he barked.

He closed the door behind us and ordered me to undress. I stood frozen watching him as he grabbed pieces of rope from a drawer in his nightstand.

"You owe me, boy! Now, do as I say and everything will be fine."

He dropped his suspenders and slowly crept toward me. My eyes dropped to the rope in his hand. Flashbacks of the basement plagued my mind, sending shockwaves throughout my body. The hair on my neck stood up as I backed up into his nightstand.

"Turn, boy."

My body was not of my control. My mind was active, but my mind was repeating the sequence. I turned from him now, facing a glass ashtray with a barely lit cigarette burning atop his nightstand. He motioned to tie my hands together but dropped the rope. My eyes peered at the ashtray once more noticing his slow reach for the dropped rope. My hand quickly grabbed at the ashtray, but the black fog settled in.

This is you, Lyle. This is who you are. Remember who you are.

These words repeated in my mind over and over again while the fog drifted from the surface. But these were not my thoughts. The voice was not of mine. It was unfamiliar and ominous.

When the fog lifted, I surveyed the scene. Dropping my chin, Wyatt's body came into view, lying unconscious, blood seeping from a wound atop his head. I dropped the remaining piece of the glass in my hand and ran out of the door, but the fog consumed me.

"Lyle, this gala is important to me. The who's who of all my clients will be there. You need to look your best." Charles's voice faintly echoed. The room fell into view, Charles standing in front of a mirror tying his bow tie.

I turned around to see the party coming into focus. I was dressed in a tailored black tuxedo, a piece of clothing a poor boy from Pennsylvania would have never imagined wearing. Charles was motioning me to greet the visitors with him. As I was walking toward him that familiar musky smell hit my nose. I glanced over my shoulder to see Wyatt Halver staring at me.

"It's so great to see you, Lyle. And in with Charles Wallace now, are we? Well, aren't you lucky." He sneered.

Wanting to avoid confrontation, I turned away from him, wanting to return to Charles but felt a tug at my arm.

"If you tell anyone what happened, and I mean anyone, boy, I will kill you and Charles. Do you understand me, boy?"

His tight grip on my arm intensified.

I yanked my arm back and turned to walk toward Charles while the room dissolved into darkness.

A familiar door appeared in front of me. I knew where I was. Or where I was heading next. I scanned my right arm for the gun I knew would be there. Charles's revolver.

Remember who you are, Lyle.

I pushed the door open and walked through. Wyatt was there, a drunken mess slobbering on his couch facing toward the fire. I walked up and cocked the gun.

He submissively moved to the bedroom where I ordered him to strip. I found the same rope in his nightstand and hogtied him. I removed my belt. With each lash, his skin melted off like butter, whipping him into a near unconscious state. Exhausted but satisfied, I pulled the gun back out of my waistband, lifting it to his head. I took one last view and pulled the trigger.

The blood spewed onto my face, bathing me into a feeling of euphoria. I reached down and traced the bullet hole with my blood stained fingers. I drank in the moment, relishing it, allowing the peace to settle in.

But the peace was temporary as I was transcended again.

"Mr. Wallace, we found your client Wyatt Halver murdered last night."

"In God's name, how?"

"Armed robbery from the looks of it. His watch and some cash were stolen. But the scene, the scene—was Mr. Halver a man of peculiar taste?"

"I don't quite understand, Chief, what is it you're getting at?" Charles furrowed his brow, perplexed. "Well, sir, he, Mr. Halver that is, was hog-tied and . . . disrobed. If he had some peculiar sexual preferences, I can assure you we can keep that from the report," Chief Wilson assured.

"Christ. Yes, yes. Leave him with some sense of decency. Even if he was a dreadful man in life."

Charles brought his hands to his face to hide his embarrassment.

"Of course, sir."

Chief Wilson nodded, then bowed out of the room.

"Christ. I can't say I'm surprised. The enemies he made, the lies he told, it was only a matter of time before someone knocked him off. Anyway, are you ready for the meeting today? We have lunch with the mayor at two and—"

My limp body smashed against the floor causing a sudden rush of head aching but was quickly overwhelmed by the pulsation of pain from my bleeding wrists and heels. As I lie there, a sudden rush of icy water sent my body an unwelcoming jolt.

"Mr. Lyle, you are still with us! Excellent. Rest up, I will be with you in a few hours for a post-treatment evaluation. Richard, grab and escort Mr. Lyle back to his room please."

Dr. Holmes's voice echoed in my mind as I was dragged to my room.

I flopped onto my bed and the door shut behind me.

CHAPTER THIRTEEN

"LYLE! LYLE! GET YER ASS up, boy! It's time," Dick said, as he lightly slapped my face mockingly.

Where am I? Am I really here? Christ, I can't even tell anymore.

Peeking my right eye open, I confirmed Dick was physically there. My hand reached back to the crank in my neck. A mountain of sweat had piled against my skin. Still lying prone.

"Now boy! Let's go. I haven't all day!" Dick growled pulling me by the back of my neck.

"Alright, alright, I'm awake. Give me just a moment to get dressed, would you?"

Frustrated, I searched for my clothes as I hadn't noticed I was still disrobed.

"Well, hurry up! The Doc has more than just you to see today!"

He struck a blow to my lower back, causing me to collapse, shirt over my head. I rushed forward, knocking my head into the concrete wall, sending me into a tailspin of dizziness. The biting cold of the concrete floor protruded through my trousers as my knees hit the floor. My head fell forward, pressing lazily into my chest. This current world was falling in and out of view.

The desolate, freezing environment slowly amend into a warm and cozy room. I could hear faint sound of music playing and the crackling of a fire nearby.

"Lyle, I know it's only been less than a year since I have taken you in, but I wanted to give you this. Here."

My eyes flickered open and shut, Charles's figure walking toward me with a box.

"This watch is a Rolex Oyster, waterproof they say. The very best. It better be for the price!" He laughed. "I know you often get confused with time and are often late," Charles heckled, slapping me on my back, "so I hope this helps remedy the situation a bit." The warmth and love emanated from his voice, nearly choking him up.

He wasn't an affectionate man, some may have even called him callous, polite in appearance but cruel in tactics, ruthless even. But as a young boy yearning for a father, he was all I had. Long gone were the days of beatings or reprehensible men. At this moment, I felt like his son.

Charles bent down and handed me the watch. The watches texture was very real as if this was really happening again. I was in this moment. I wanted to stay here forever.

I studied its beauty and was amazed, all over again. Charles gave me many things, but I knew this watch meant something. This memory was cherished to me. Yet, I seemed to have forgotten all about it.

"I do hope you like it. As you know, I never had the chance to be a father, well a real father."

He stopped, letting the words sit in the air, trying to keep himself together.

"With Maryanne gone as well, you're all the family I have left. I know you have had a rough go at life. Me too." He paused again.

"But I hope this Christmas that you feel things are improving, my boy."

Charles pressed his hand on my shoulder affectionally and walked out of the room, sniffling. The memory slowly dissolved in the crackling of the fire.

"You moron! Now look at what you have done! You have potentially squandered my assessment and the results! How am I to observe him looking like this? Is he bleeding? Good Lord, he is!"

Rang the distant screams of Dr. Holmes. A smacking sound reverberated off the walls, catching my attention.

"I'm sorry, sir, he was just, he was taking too long and I wanted to hurry him up a bit. I didn't mean to knock him senseless." Dick quivered.

"Well pick him up and bring him to my office, I'll try to bring him around and do my best under these horrendous conditions. And don't you dare lay another blow on him, do you understand me? Or so help me you will be back in here too!" Dr. Holmes barked at Dick.

Back? Is this real? Or is this too a dream?

My body was slumped over Dick's shoulder my head bouncing with each step he took. My mind must've longed for an escape. Dredging up old memories, some cruel and painful, but this one I want to return to forever.

But I could still feel the imprint of the watch in my hands, I could smell the pine in the air. I could still see the snow blanketing the ground outside the window. The fire roaring after Riley, Charles's assistant, offered more wood to keep the apartment cozy and bearable. Those senses were just as real as this. My mind drifted back to that memory, floating between reality and the past.

"Sir, you should get ready, Mr. Wallace will be expecting you downstairs with the guests soon. Your favorite eggnog is ready for you as well. Would you like me to bring it to you?" Riley politely gestured.

"No, no thank you, I'll be down in a moment."

My eyes still spellbound by the watch.

"Put him right here, right in this chair! I'll have to do an examination to make sure you didn't harm his head even more! Now leave, you fool, I can take care of the rest."

Dr. Holmes's words crept in, attempting to lure me out of the memory I was desperately clinging to.

"Everyone, everyone, this year has been one of the best for us here at Wallace and Partners. We are continuing to grow at a pace unheard of.

Hell, we are even outshining those down in Chicago!" Charles chuckled. "I just want to send my sincere gratitude to all those who are here and have helped. We have done great work here. The timing has been right, the money is in sight, and it's all for the taking!" Charles beamed.

"And to my boy, Lyle. Come here, will ya?"

I walked toward him as he situated me front and center, placing his arms atop my shoulders.

"This boy, at the age of sixteen, can you believe it? My how he has grown right before my eyes, making me an old man!" The room laughed.

"He has managed to pick up all of the workings as quickly as I once did. I couldn't be more proud."

My eyes fell to the floor, a lump developing in my throat.

"Now, there's booze and eggnog in the other room. Just don't tell anyone!" He whispered jokingly.

"Go, go, have fun, and Merry Christmas to all!"

The memory drifted. This time for good.

"Mr. Lyle. Can you hear me? Your eyes are welling up. Grief, how is that head of yours? I've cleaned up your wound there. You were bleeding in extraordinary amounts. But, the head does typically bleed in loads. Can you hear me? I have a post-assessment I would like to complete and I need your full cooperation. Mr. Lyle?"

Dr. Holmes snapped his fingers in my face, awaking me back to his office.

CHAPTER FOURTEEN

"GOOD, GOOD. LET ME LOOK at your eyes."

He walked up and peered into my open eyes, causing them to dry up.

"Ah, you seem to be coming back to us now. Good. Good. Well, Mr. Lyle, welcome back!"

Blinking away the wet eyes, my eyes focused in regaining my sight. Dr. Holmes stood a few feet from me. His hands clasped together in excitement as he walked around an oak desk back to his chair. The desk was absolutely meticulous, looking as if it was waxed regularly. Not a paper or pen out of place.

"I know our first sit-down was, interesting to say the least. So I wanted to make it up to you and have a real discussion, man to man. Here we are now, and I couldn't be any more thrilled!" His vile grin gleamed.

"Mhmm."

I was still coming to.

"A man of few words I see. Just as when you entered here. Fascinating. But you seem to be a man of words with, Mr. Lancaster, is it? The cripple in the chair. How did that strange acquaintance come about?"

"What are you biting at?"

"I'm simply asking a question. Mr. Lancaster and you are vastly different, wouldn't you say? I wouldn't exactly have pegged you for friends beforehand. A man such as yourself doesn't have many friends, is that right?"

"I have found good is far and few. It's best to catch it when it comes." I retorted.

"Because you have met some ghastly creatures haven't you?"

I pursed my lips together, unsure of what to say.

"Mr. Lyle, please do be frank. This is not a deposition and you are no longer on stand. The trial is over. You are with me until I release you back to the penitentiary. I can deem you competent today and send you on your way back to the federal penitentiary. Where were you headed? Was it Rikers? Alcatraz? I can imagine those options aren't exactly appealing, now are they?" He sneered.

Disinterested in his words, I lifted my head to stare at the painting behind him. It was fascinating. A mighty ship nearly capsized by the hurling wave lunging toward it. Yet, it was fighting to remain. The clouds were unforgiving but somehow looked as if the storm was nearing its end. The artwork here intrigues me unlike any other I had ever seen in galleries back in New York.

Dr. Holmes peered at me, then turned his head to see what I was captivated over.

"Ah yes, it's marvelous isn't it? Spellbinding."

I exhaled.

"A metaphor, I suppose, for where we are today. Each of us, tempted by fate, luring us into the mightiest of desperate oceans. Some of us capsize. Others, well, are like the ship. Staying steadfast, despite the pressure. Awaiting the clearing of the tumultuous clouds. Which of the two are you, Mr. Lyle?"

"Does one really know?"

"Fascinating! Tell me more!" He leaned in, ready to hang on every word.

I exhaled again. My eyes turning back to the painting.

"Well let's start at the beginning and you can fill me in with some missing details. Of course, all of this is pure speculation. None of this will be recorded. Absolutely and purely between you and me."

"Why are you here?" was all I muttered. My soul isn't ready for any retrospective into who I was.

"Me? Where? At Price State Institute? Well, of course I'm here to guide people, such as yourself, back to some sense of normality. Although, this can be a rather difficult feat with the increasingly disturbed. But I find myself to be quite the *specialist*," he said the last in a French accent, almost humoring himself, cracking a slight grin.

"Why madness? Why not become a *real* doctor?"

My condescension and disgust lingered.

"Your distaste for me is quite clear, Mr. Lyle. But I hold no grudges, I promise. I'm here to simply identify how you became the supposed 'monster' they claim you to be. Now please cooperate, I have carved out some time for you, but I do have a treatment tonight that I must attend to. Are you ready?"

I scratched my face with my right hand, raising my shoulders.

A soft knock echoed behind me.

"Come in. Ah yes, absolute timing! Wonderful. Please, set them here. Thank you, Allie."

Through the corner of my eyes, I could see a young woman entering in with a tray of cups. Her white attire accented her lovely skin. The light danced around here, propelling her fair complexion and red lips. Her brown curls flowed down her ears, meeting at her shoulders. Her beauty resembled a young Clara, innocent and naïve but pure. My eyes never left her as she placed the two cups and saucers on the desk. Her twinkling brown eyes beamed at me momentarily, sparking a forgotten feeling.

"That'll be all, Allie. You can go."

He shooed her as he caught wave of my interest.

"Beautiful creature, isn't she? So young, so pure. Innocent. Uncorrupted." He nearly salivated.

I sat back in the chair, perched higher than before.

"I hope you don't mind, I enjoy a nice, hot, refreshing cup of coffee with each assessment. In a quite auspicious turn of events, I had one brought for you as well! Voila!"

He lifted the cup and saucer and placed it before me on the desk. A devilish grin widened on his face.

"Madness, my dear, is purely subjective. I, in particular, enjoy getting lost in it. Let's enter into your madness, Mr. Lyle."

He brought the coffee to his lips and sipped.

I stared down at the coffee in front of me. The steam poked at my face. Inviting me in. It has been such a time since I've had the taste. Wasn't always enthused with the taste prior, but now, I crave the bitterness. I could see him staring at me, awaiting my first sip. His eagerness was deafening.

"It won't bite. I promise. It's quite exquisite, if I may say so myself."

He put the cup down on the saucer, folding his hands on the desk, ready for me to relent.

A resurgence of thirst quelled my mind. I reached for the cup feeling the weight of the liquid in my right hand. I brought the cup to my nose and was enthralled with the smell. The liquid was frighteningly searing but a warm reminder of what life there is outside of this glacial hell.

The taste was bitter but invigorating. Despite the temperature, I continued to drink more and more, yearning for every last drop. The emptiness weighed down on me once the last drop was drank.

"Ah, good, wasn't it?"

He smiled.

"I'm glad you enjoyed it. There are few joys in this life, so we must savor them all."

He pressed the cup to his lips to drink another sip, the aroma striking a deepening thirst.

He placed the cup back onto the saucer.

"How old were you when you left home, quite young I presume?"

I sat back into the chair, my eyes turning away from his.

"Oh, come, come. It is quite apparent that Mr. Wallace was not, in fact, your biological father. He was a man of austerity, you are crass. No amount of teaching can wipe away the stench of lower class. Also, Lyle is your surname. James is your legal name. *James Lyle*. Why have you forsaken your forename?"

He leaned in, placing his left hand on his lower lip.

I lifted my head and turned back to the painting.

"Oh come, come, Mr. Lyle. You can stop with the act."

My eyes walked back to his.

"I know a great deal about you. I know you are a man of high emotional instability. *The real you*. You *remember who you are, don't you*? Because *I know you*."

"You don't know me." I scoffed, fists clenching.

"Oh, but don't I?"

He turned away from me, pulling a file from the top cabinet, flopping it onto his desk.

"This, this is a history, rather detailed and extensive, I admit, from Dr. Price. Of you."

He paused, pointing at me.

"The voices you have heard, the men you have killed. Gunshots, stabbings, even the one that garnered your nickname, 'Hangman,' all of it. Here. Right here. All of you, condensed down to one file. Here in my drawer. Top spot."

He folded his hands on top of each other, shoulders erect.

"You must've known? No? Well, not as clever as you think yourself to be."

I palmed the table in frustration, motioning for him to lay it all out.

"As you may already know, Dr. Price, of Price State Institute, genius of a man, was a dear friend of Mr. Wallace. Mr. Wallace was rather concerned with how your increased drinking and shall we say, drug use turned into intensive nightmares. Screaming and talking indecipherably to yourself at night. Quite the fright, even for me!"

He leaned in.

"He was *more* than concerned, Mr. Lyle. You were to be committed. Shocking? The betrayal?"

"Mhmm."

"But, Mr. Wallace, again, wasn't your *real* father, so what could be expected? Who *is* your *real* father, Mr. Lyle?"

I lifted my finger to my temple, pretending to think. Then shrug my shoulders.

"Ah, again, interesting that you *choose* to be called by your surname. Why not *James*? Perhaps this was your *real* fathers name? Hmm? Simmering issues stemming from adolescence?"

I rubbed my left hand across my lower face. Words had yet to leave my lips.

"Your father, was he abusive, perhaps?"

I absentmindedly rolled my shoulders forward, uncomfortable in this wooden chair, favoring my right side, away from Dr. Holmes.

He examined my body movements and brought himself closer in the chair.

"In these beatings, did you ever, at any time, fantasize about killing him? The merciless punishments. Endless beatings. It must've crossed your mind to be rid of him? Any sane individual would want this, no?"

Silence deafened.

"Mr. Lyle, or is it *James*?" He snickered.

"It is perfectly normal to wish death on a person inflicting torturous conditions. In fact, it would be quite abnormal to *not* want to." He playfully laughed.

"Now James. James, can you tell me—"

"Lyle. It's Lyle," I interjected.

"Right, James, can you—"

"Goddamn you, it's Lyle!"

I ascended up from my chair, slamming my fists against the desk, ready to pounce. Towering over him, I could see the eagerness and excitement pour into his eyes, beaming.

"Marvelous, Mr. Lyle! Marvelous!"

He clasped his hands together, pressing them in his chest as he swarmed his body back into the chair.

"I believe we have made some headway today! I truly believe we—"

Another knock hit the door. Much deeper and louder than before. A familiar voice belted through.

"Sir," nearly breathless, "come. We are having an issue with Beast! Come! Quick!"

Dick hurried to Dr. Holmes, widened eyes protruding. Something was amiss. The look of panic was discernable and apparent.

Without saying a word, he rose up and hurried through the door. Dick had missed me in the commotion but had now made contact with my eyes.

"Fuck! Always in the Goddamn way. Follow me! I have no time to take you back to your space. If you try to run, I'll cripple you worse than your friend! Now move it!"

He pulled me up by my collar and rushed me through the door. Where we were going, I was unsure. But the panic of both Dick and Dr. Holmes had me relishing every second.

CHAPTER FIFTEEN

"HOW DID THIS HAPPEN? *WHO* let this happen? Goddamn it! I need some answers now!"

Dr. Holmes barked into Dick face as we approached the open cell door. This one was different than mine. The door was a cell with open bars that allowed full viewing access. The hallway was home to only this cell. It was spacious but empty. There was no bed, just a blanket and a sheet on the concrete floor. The cold flowed freely down here, sending a whirl of chills. Darkness engulfed the backside of the cell. Conditions were fraught for even an animal.

"Where's George? He was to be tending to Mr. Harold."

Dr. Holmes threw up his right hand and wiped his face.

"I . . . I dunno. I found, found this."

Dick bent down and grabbed the lantern on the floor, bringing it to the back of the cell.

"Dear God! We must find him immediately! Did you call the Inspector?"

Dr. Holmes turned away, rushing out of the cell, holding his stomach in disgust.

I slowly walked forward, hoping to catch a glimpse. As I approached near, I could see it. The light casted from the lantern danced over the walls, exposing a stark red. The recognizable salty smell was ripe in the air. I inhaled, closing my eyes, taking in that familiar aroma.

"Good Lord, George has to be dead by the looks of this monstrosity. Has his body been recovered?"

Dr. Holmes was still holding his stomach, motioning farther from the smell.

"Almost."

Dick buried his head into his chest, barely able to mutter these words as Dr. Holmes flew into a fury.

"Almost! Almost? What does that even mean?"

He grabbed Dick by the collar of his jacket.

"Whatever wasn't eaten, whatever was intact was recovered and placed in the morgue. It's not much."

Dick hesitated.

"Good Lord! Lyle? Why is Lyle here?" Dr. Holmes turned toward me. "Get him out of here, now! Now, I say!"

Dick grabbed me by my collar and started to drag me out of the hallway. I shrugged off his grip and walked forward, turning to look back at Dr. Holmes. Breaking through the cracks of my face was a smile. A twinkle was felt in my eye and a spring was in my step. I faced forward, pleased at what I had seen and continued down the hallway.

CHAPTER SIXTEEN

"GO ON! GET IN."

Dick pushed me in my room, slamming the door behind him, leaving me to barely catch my balance before another tumble occurred. My face was tickled by my wavy hair reaching past my eyebrows. I hadn't realized how long it was getting. It feels like ages since I have had a haircut. I brushed back my hair from my face and felt the grease run through my fingers.

I'm a mess. The least they could offer is a bath.

I wiped my hands on my trousers and noticed there was something off in the room. Something, everything just didn't feel quite right. I froze in my tracks, my eyes scanning the room, still adjusting from the vivid lights of the hallway.

The room was unusually darker than normal. Instead of a semblance of light protruding under the doorway, darkness engulfed my senses, blurring the lines of a dream or reality. A sudden weight drooped over me. My eyes motioned upward, and I immediately understood what was wrong. The entity was here.

In the corner, above my bed, there he perched, blue eyes glowing through the darkness, glaring me down. It seemed larger than I had previously perceived.

I observed, mesmerized, terrified, and bewildered.

The silence roared in the background. The usually freezing room was neither cold nor hot, it just was. I felt as if the moment was on a loop of a consistent silence, never deviating. It was maddening. The eyes never broke their stare and I didn't dare. As long as I was watching it, I knew where it was. In a sense, I feared this entity for I am unsure of its desires, but for that same reason, I loathe it. I need to know.

"What do you want? What do you want from *me*?" I bellowed.

Silence.

The tension was unnerving. Thick in the air was uncertainty. But I was determined to get something, anything. I needed to know if I was going mad or if this was my reality. My *new* reality.

I inched closer, careful in my approach. I wondered if I moved too quickly, would it interpret it as a threat? If I moved too slowly, would it wonder if I was terrified?

Does it know what I am thinking? Can it read my thoughts?

I picked up my right foot to take another step but was struck with a lightening of pain traveling from my back to the top of my head. The pain thundered viciously, dropping me to my knees. I desperately clung the back of my head in my hands. I squeezed my eyes shut, burying my head into my lap in complete agony. The piercing scream slowly crept up, then leaped into my ears, overtaking the striking pain in my head. A visual of Elbert echoed in my mind.

"Why are you doing this? I see them, I see them all! Please, please, stop! I can't—" was all I could scream out as the image of Elbert replayed. I could see him on his knees, pleading, begging for his life, just as I was doing now.

I stood over him with the revolver in my right hand, his Bible still in his left, and a smirk on my face. I cocked the revolver, watching him close his eyes as a worried sweat rested on his forehead. He tucked his head into his chest, clasping his hands together in prayer.

"Your God no longer hears you."

I bent down and whipped him with the revolver, smearing a heap of blood onto the butt of the gun. He groaned in agony, wallowing on his back, holding his distorted nose. His hands cleansed in the vibrant red. I smacked his hands away from his nose, allowing the waterfall to immerse my own hands. I dipped my finger into the pool of blood, making the sign of the cross on his forehead. His welted green eyes stared up one last time as I pulled the gun back out from my waistband, firing between his eyes. He fell back. The sound of his head cracked against the concrete steps. Pulling a cigarette from my coat, I bent down to stare at him, salivating in my cigarette, taking in the fraught chill of an early fall.

I stood back up, glaring at him one last time, dropping the Bible on his chest before I turned and walked away.

"He was a terrible man, all he had done, he, he deserved it!"

I mustered a breathy reply to the creature.

Elbert's open eyes were a constant visual in my mind. I had nearly forgotten about this man through the chaos of the time. This was years ago.

Why am I seeing this? All of this?

Then the unfamiliar voice sounded in my head.

Remember who you are. You will remember . . .

"I know who I am! I know exactly—"

The torture let up and I fell back, exhausted and dazed, lying on the cold floor looking up. My racing heart was a welcome sign to know I was still alive. I gazed up but noticed the creature had disappeared. A bright flash of light stunned my eyes, covering them; I felt a heavy kick to my shoulder.

CHAPTER SEVENTEEN

"GET UP! GET UP, FREAK! I brought y'er food."

Dick dropped the food tray onto my bed, spilling some of the rice on the sheet. I shook loose of the prior moment and wiped my eyes, feeling a crust as if I had been sleeping.

Dick scoffed as he looked down at me on the floor wiping my eyes. I could see him turning to walk away.

"Did you catch him yet?"

"Who?" Dick questioned?

"The one you called Beast?" Did you catch him yet?" A smile unknowingly melted onto my face.

"Oh, yer think this is amusing do ya? A man gets skinned alive and your laughing. What kind of sick freak are ya?"

His voice shook halfway through the sentence.

"Skinned, huh? That's how old George went, did he?" I could feel my smile widen.

I had no ill will with George but seeing Dr. Holmes and Dick so shaken up was worth more to me in the moment.

"You think you are a really funny character, don't you? Sitting in here, guarded by these doors now. Let's see you out there with him like I was, let's see you."

"Let's, then."

I rose to my feet, wiping off the dirt from my clothes, straightening myself out before I dredged my eyes into his.

I could see his right fist tightening up, sweat beading on his hairline.

"Oh, come on, Dick, what's the matter? A little blood have you squeamish?"

I raised my right hand under my chin and crossed my left to my chest, admiring his fear, soaking it in, every last drop. I audibly inhaled the moment, letting him know that danger was not a past tense word for me. It existed heavily in the present. What do I have to lose any how?

"Sick son of a bitch! I hope he kills ya! Ya deserved the Goddamn chair. What he sees in ya, I'll never understand. I'da killed you long ago."

He backed up, a quiver shaking in his voice. He quickly turned around and slammed the door behind him.

As the door shut, reality set back in, reminding me I was alone in this hell. It dawned on me that I hadn't heard from Tommy in some time. I wondered if he was doing fine.

A tear welled in my left eye as I looked down at the tray on my bed. I hadn't eaten in so long that I disregarded hunger. I sat on the bed stuffing the food into my face but savoring the water in the cup on the floor. It wasn't much, but it was something I needed to keep me going.

I finished with my tray and walked it to the front of the door, setting it down as I finished off the last drops of water from my cup. I turned back to my bed and noticed the book I had grabbed some time back when I was given access to the library.

I walked over and dropped to my right knee, picking up the book, relieved. In the faint of the light, the title shone through the withered cover: *Frankenstein by Mary Shelley*. I flipped through the pages to the end, basking in the smell of the old leather bound book.

Admiring the book, the age added a wisdom and life experience of a past unseen but still felt. I sighed a sense of relief. Finally, a world I can get lost in that wasn't of my own. I grabbed the sheet from the bed and walked back near the door, utilizing the faint light. Sliding down the wall,

I wrapped the sheet around me and opened the book. The crinkle of the page was a sweet delight, so few awarded to me.

Page one.

I began to read, devouring every page and washing myself in the world of another. But I stopped, set the book on my lap, leaving it open on the page I had left off on and rested my head to the wall.

Nothing.

I sighed in relief.

Absolutely nothing. I chuckled at this sense of momentary peace. It was refreshing and gave me a sense of a breath I hadn't felt in some time. A relief in the wilderness I had been condemned to for so long.

I peered into the darkness to see only that, darkness. I shook my head in delight retrieving the novel, continuing in my journey.

> *Even broken in spirit as he is, no one can feel more deeply than he does the beauties in nature. . . . Such a man has a double existence: he may suffer misery, and be overwhelmed by disappointments; yet when he has retired into himself, he will be like a celestial spirit, that has a halo around him, within whose circle no grief or folly ventures.*

I wallowed in the darkness. The misery of the broken spirited is my existence.

CHAPTER EIGHTEEN

I AWOKE TO FIND MYSELF shivering on the bone-chilling floor. I squinted my eyes open to take notice of my surroundings. The book had fallen over in my lap as my head pressed against the wall. The sheet had fallen from my shoulders to my lap, exposing me to the cold.

I rubbed at my eyes and took in a sigh of relief. No creature, no noises, just pure silence. A state of serenity lifted me to my feet as I walked back to sit on my bed. I lifted the book to my eyes to take another look at the little piece of joy I had left. I relished in the thought of continuing in my journey into a world that wasn't my own. I took one final look at the book, then set it down on the floor next to my bed. True monsters are made from men who create them.

I laid my head to the bed and took in another breath. Peace still flowed freely. I could almost hear a sonata wistfully playing in the background— in fact, its beautiful melodies culminating.

My mind moved to the theatre as the pianist flowed from one note to the other, connecting the sound of the song to the music in my heart. The piano continued playing an easy listening tempo, soothing me to a dream state.

The melodies flowed through my mind seamlessly, without hesitation, without judgment. The warmth of music brought me back to a feeling of sincere life.

"Isn't he just marvelous? What a spectacular night, my boy!"

Charles whispered in, gleaming at me as Gershwin's Rhapsody in Blue echoed for the first time. I had never been to a live musical performance before. Aeolian Hall was a true wonder. The space was large enough to hold an entire symphony, yet intimate enough to spotlight a sitting artist alone at the keys.

"He's wonderful. This, this is all wonderful."

I took in the moment, radiating happiness. Gershwin continued playing in the background. I remember looking over at Charles as he sat to my left. His hazel eyes fixated forward, lost in the melody of the performance. He held his hands up to his lips, only removing them for an applause. He looked elegant in his tailored black suit. His silky wavy black hair with a touch of white only added to his grace.

I remember trying to imitate his slicked back hair early in our relationship. He would take the comb and laugh, "You must find your own way," then he would hand me back the comb as I would comb it right back. He smelled of a sweet musk, never overbearing but always noticeable. This is the Charles I will hold true to me.

As the last song played and the final note was heard, I turned to Charles to see a tear streaming down his face. At first, I was unsettled by his so very open and public display of emotion. But he wasn't. He was sure of himself and let himself feel, openly and honestly. He pulled the handkerchief out of his jacket pocket and dabbed at the tear, reflecting a warm smile to me, and we stood in ovation at the masterpiece we all had heard. Although the music had finished, the music never truly stopped playing in my heart.

"Lyle, you need to wake up now."

I was confused as Charles had turned to speak to me to wake up.

"What do you mean?"

I was puzzled. I didn't want this to end.

"Lyle, you need to wake up!"

Charles screamed at me and my eyes forced themselves open, jolting me awake. The room was no longer dark and I could see a sight above me. The icy-blue eyes had returned, and they were hovering. The cold dead-eyed stare brought me back to the reality of where I was. Hell hath no patience for the wicked.

My heartbeat slowly crept up, beating faster and faster with each moment that I was becoming fully cognizant of. As close as we were, I was sure I was to die. I had never seen these eyes so close and so cold, callous, and wrought with malevolence. My twisted, distorted face, watching me, it was nearly more than I could handle.

I have never been a praying man, but as I looked up, I considered if I should become one.

I stared back at the eyes one last time, taking a deep inhale, bracing for what would be next. Death was imminent. It is always imminent. We are born to die. My mind had run tired of the continuous bouts of fear I had been met with. The sonata rang through my ears once more as my body let go and sank into the bed.

"Mr. Lyle!"

Fingers snapped in my face, pulling me back from my state. Started, I opened my eyes, looking up to see the blue eyes of Dr. Holmes starting back down at me.

CHAPTER NINETEEN

"MR. LYLE, MR.—AH YES, YOU are awake now. Marvelous! Would you mind getting dressed and coming with me, I have a little trip I'd like to take with you. Come quickly now."

He turned and walked out of the room as a pair of trousers and a fresh shirt were left on my bed. Curiously, the door was propped open. The light rang in like a ray of sunshine, nearly blinding me.

I sat up and gazed around the room. A mouse dashed from the corner, startling me. I lifted the sheet from my body and pressed my feet against the floor. The cold biting at my heels was reminiscent of walking barefoot in a snowy field.

I picked up the trousers and noticed some sock garments had been left, although riddled with holes and unsightly, I eagerly covered my feet and rejoiced in the warmth. Something was better than nothing. Once more, I pressed my feet to the floor and stood, inserting one leg at a time into these trousers, sending a memory back to the first time I was fitted for a real suit.

"Sir, you have to stand still now. I cannot take proper measurements with you moving about. Now please, stand still," ordered Joseph Geoffrey, Charles's personal tailor. He was a rude man, audacious and particular. Joseph was an older man, nearing his fifties, perhaps, silvery blonde hair that parted heavy on the right. A hair never out of place nor a wrinkle in his suit. A round fella, but he carried it well. He wore what he made, the absolute best. Always endowed with a handkerchief to match the tie he wore. Today was a velvet red.

"You will have entered here a poor ragged boy but will leave a man fitted like a true king!"

He praised as the fitting completed, clasping his hands together then turned back to write the full measurements on his scrapbook. Hundreds of men, powerful and wealthy, lined that book. Addresses and names of New York's finest visited him. Yet here I am. Here I *was*.

"Hold on a minute, you are going to need these shoes, put 'em on. Hurry now would ya?"

Dick handed me some brown lace up boots. My calloused feet were relieved to finally get a reprieve. I grabbed the shoes and sat back on the bed, unlacing the shoes then placing my feet in them. It felt foreign yet familiar. Walking barefoot became a staple, normal even. Having shoes on again felt bizarre, but I embraced the moment and stood up in them, appreciating every second I felt as a normal being.

I walked toward the door enjoying the feeling of the boots hitting the ground despite my feet swimming in them. I was dubious of the motives or where I was headed, but for the slightest chance to feel "normal" again, I savored it.

"It's about time!"

Dick closed my door as I walked out of the room into the hallway. He grabbed my arm and squeezed, pulling me into him as we met face-to-face.

"Now look here, no funny business, do ya hear? Nothing at all. If you try anything so help me—"

"You'll do what?" I scoffed and pulled my arm from his grip. "Lead the way." I motioned to him opening my right arm.

He walked up to me, peered into my eyes, then walked forward.

"Follow me, then," he snubbed.

Walking down the hallway, I examined the rooms. With each room we passed, I looked for Tommy. I hadn't the faintest idea how long it had been since we last spoke but I knew I needed to see him again. I needed to know he was alright.

As we entered a new hallway, the lights faded and the temperature sank. As George's room was open with bars, so to were these. I came up to this room on the right. The back corners were dark, but I could hear a whimpering emanating from the darkness. My curiosity got the better of me as I maneuvered closer to the bars, slowing my pace to catch a glimpse of what was in there. As I got closer, I could see a person, bare with long black hair rocking in the corner facing the wall. The room stunk of urine and feces. The smell was revolting. I looked over at Dick to see him stopped and laughing under his hand over his mouth.

"You think you are the only freak around here? I think this one has you topped!"

He laughed as he tried to hold back his disgust. My stomach burbled from the smell, but I couldn't leave. I needed to get closer. I needed to see this . . . person.

As I inched closer, nearing the door, the whimpering stopped, almost as if it knew I was there without looking. I paused, unsure of what may happen. I looked to my left and noticed Dick was gone. The hallway lights started to flicker. I turned back to the cell and saw *him*. He frightened me, sending me a few steps back. He was standing there at the doorway of the gate, staring back at me through the bars. His hair was long and coarse, reaching past his scarred shoulders. Much of his body was torn from what looked like beatings and afflictions. Tears and scars littered his emaciated body. His complexion was hardly visible as he resembled a man who had once lived but had now been dead for some time. He did not move nor did he blink. A word was not released from his lips. But his black eyes swallowed me hole as his stare intensified.

A low growl stemmed from the room but I could not distinguish if he was the one making the noise. I watched, unsettled at his unsightly appearance. As I tilted my head to study him, he tilted his. When I moved closer, he did as well. He mirrored me in my actions but never said a word. My eyes widened and my shoulders hunched, my body leaning into itself, nervous. I tried to fight a rising panic but it was in the air, palpable and real.

These metal bars, these rooms, they are different from mine. Tommy was in a room similar to mine, but this . . . "man"—this "Beast"—is caged in here, with open viewing, alone and in the dark. A shiver ran down my spine at the thought of being locked on this side too.

As the thought entered my mind, a smile widened on his face. His yellow-stained teeth illustrated razor-like teeth. It's as if he had sharpened them purposely. His nose was crooked, leaning more to his right then his left. A slice of skin looked to be missing on his left side of his cheek directly under his eyes. The scar had been played with, looking to have been infected several times. It was uncomfortable looking at him. My hands were cold and clammy. I had seen evil before but never like this. He was *real*.

"What did I tell you about no funny business? Follow me now before ya get yourself killed! You think these bars are here for pretty? Why do you think his cell is open? We watch him all day! Smarten up, boy!"

Dick smacked me upside my head. But I didn't react, too afraid to turn away from what was.

"You think you're something, huh? Well, let me tell you, you haven't even touched the surface here!"

Dick grabbed my arm and pulled me away. I couldn't move myself. I was frozen. Stuck against my will. He lifted his boney finger and pointed at me. He mouthed an inaudible "You" to me, then smiled; his eyes never wavering from mine. I was pulled out of the hallway and his smile never relented. As I turned the corner, I could still feel his eyes on the back of my head.

CHAPTER TWENTY

THESE HALLS SEEM ENDLESS, A maze certainly. A sick and demented labyrinth highlighting how creatures' nightmares are formed. That smile of the "man" has plagued me since we left the hallway; I cannot seem to get it out of my head. The image skulks and haunts, it was unsightly and gruesome. I've never seen a smile look so malevolent. My body shuddered at the thought of coming face-to-face with him once more.

Wandering in these halls, in Dick's shadow, the realization that I do not belong here grows. I have few regrets in this life but pleading insanity was a misstep. Rikers, hell, even Alcatraz, cannot compare to the Devil's architectural playground situated right here. It's almost quite funny. At one moment in time, I felt fearless, untouchable, ruthless, yet here I am today, afraid of those confined with me and what lurks in the night.

"We're here, now do something with your hair and yer face ya freak."

Dick stopped me, pushing his hand into my chest just before we reached this familiar door, handing me a damp wet towel to wipe my face. The towel was cold, but I poured my face into it and began to wash off. The feeling was exuberant. Having a proper bath seemed like ages ago. I could feel myself escaping from under the pits of the rubble. After wiping my face and my neck, I stared back at the towel to see it had blackened from the dirt having had collected on my face. I felt my face with my hand and could feel a beard growing, but it felt free and breathable. I extended my hand with the towel to Dick.

"I need to shave ya. You look like hell."

"No." I stood stern.

"I sure as hell can't trust you with a razor. It'll be quick and painless. Now sit right there, the table has some supplies. Hurry, now, we have to be quick!"

Dick motioned me to the table a few steps away with a bowl of water, some lather and a brush, and a wooden chair to sit.

I was leery of him but deeply wanted this beard removed from my face. Relenting, I sat in the chair and let him quickly shave me. To my surprise, not a single groove, nor did he slice my throat.

"Now, walk through that door. Hurry now. Go on!"

I looked over at the door a few steps away. An exit. It was the same door I entered when I arrived inside the asylum. The memory of passing through this door is as vibrant and rich as it was when I arrived.

Standing from the chair, I licked my fingers and glided my hands through my hair. I could feel the curls having grown to a carefree manner and wild wisps. The naturally produced oils made it easy to slick back as I hadn't washed it in God knows when. I straightened myself back out and fixed my shirt to ensure it was properly tucked in. I hadn't the faintest idea for where I was going, but to be out of this hell, even for a slight few moments, was as worthy of an occasion as ever.

Dick sneered at me and opened the door.

"Walk through, they will be waiting for ya on the other side. Go now."

He shooed me through, immediately slamming the door shut after I walked through. I could hear the immediate bolting of the door. If one dared to try an escape, that door would present a grim undertaking.

Leery in my steps, I heard a familiar sonata playing in the background. *What is this?*

I halted, taking a deep breath, admiring the artwork around me. The paintings, the statues, it was just as breathtaking as when I first viewed them. The floors glistened as they once did when I first stepped foot onto them. I turned in wonder and amazement. Standing here, outside of that confinement, I felt alive again.

A clock's bell chiming pulled me from my admiration of the sights. I looked up to see a hanging wall clock, it read six o'clock. To my right was the two-sided man once more.

"Ah, Mr. Lyle, how good of you to join us! So very good! You look well, quite well!"

I turned to see Dr. Holmes and a couple following behind him. Dr. Holmes approached, handing me a glass filled with red.

"How about some red wine, huh? An occasion such as this deserves a drink to fit the mood shall we say?"

Dr. Holmes bowed his head and turned to the couple. They were an attractive, young couple. Seemed to be no older than their early thirties, could have been mistaken for the Hollywood type. The man, resembling John Gilbert, sported a tailored cream colored tuxedo with a rubescent handkerchief, matching the dress color of the dame with him. Her pinned curly hair and perched lips reminded me of Mildred Davis as they walked in together, her arm wrapped around his.

"Mr. and Mrs. Tracey, this is the man you have been waiting for."

Dr. Holmes motioned for me to move in closer as he rested his arm around my shoulders.

"Mr. Lyle, the Tracey's, Marc and Joan. They are important benefactors of this wonderful institute. Joan's father is the Senator. He has favored this institute for decades. We hope he continues to do so, Mrs. Tracey."

Dr. Holmes patted Joan's hands, eagerly awaiting her response.

"Of course, Dr. Holmes! My father has been a huge proponent of continuing your fine work here! He favored your predecessor, Dr. Price, and has grown quite the liking to you, my dear," Joan cooed toward Dr. Holmes, making him blush.

Marc reached out his hand to mine.

"It's a pleasure to meet you, Mr. Lyle. We have been eagerly awaiting this meeting!"

I stared down at his hand before I reluctantly reached back and shook it, grabbing his forearm with my left. He looked down at my hand, uneasy but didn't fight it. I turned my eyes to his. Glaring at him, emotionless. He looked away, trying to change the mood.

"We have been in Dr. Holmes's ear for some time to see you. And now the time has come!"

He half-heartedly laughed.

"You see, we have been following your case from the start, Hangman of the Upper East. What a marvelous name, isn't it Joan?"

Joan chimed in, "So grand, so mystique!"

They belly laughed in unison, as if I was to join. I smirked and nodded cautiously.

"I hope you don't mind our prying, Mr. Lyle, but we here are obsessed with crime. We have both read countless stories and heard the tales of Jack the Ripper and other men. But to physically meet a killer, right here, in the flesh, what an absolute honor."

Marc lifted his right arm to pat my shoulder, but my glare had him thinking otherwise. He dropped his hand and ran it through the side of his hair, smiling uneasy.

His backhanded compliments were contemptuous and insulting. I took a step toward them and watched as their smiles turned to worry. A smile emerged from my face. I lifted the glass of wine from my left hand and slid all of its contents down my thirst-occupied throat, savoring the liquid as it flowed down into my belly.

"Ah. Better!"

I muttered, handing the glass back to Dr. Holmes. The room was on edge. My unpredictability had pulled them from their perceived state of ease.

"Mr. Lyle, they have traveled a long way to see you and would like to discuss a few many questions with you, if you please, have a seat so they can begin."

Dr. Holmes motioned to the couch and chairs behind us. I knew I was expected to sit in the chair, so I obliged, walking directly to, sitting back and extending my hand to motion for them to sit. I crossed my legs, relaxing into the atmosphere. A haunting smile again emerged on my face as I felt in control. The interest they claimed to have could not mask the fear arising from their bodies. A show they want, a show they shall get.

CHAPTER TWENTY-ONE

"MR. LYLE, THERE IS MUCH folklore surrounding your crimes. The police claim you have dozens of bodies buried, but they are yet to be found. Is it true that you murdered dozens of men?"

Marc gleefully looked at Joan, placing his hand on top of hers.

I glared at Marc. His previous handsome looks had deformed to a contemptuous and ignorant face. Looking at him infuriated me with each word he spewed. The smile on my face shaped into a scowl, disapproving of his line of questioning. The men I killed, this was a matter between God and me.

"Mr. Lyle, if you please, a simple answer would suffice." Dr. Holmes, who was sitting in a chair to my left, delegating like a moderator.

Joan uncrossed her legs and positioned herself toward me. "Mr. Lyle, I understand these questions can come off very personal but any information you can provide really helps in our findings. You see, we are writing a novel on our collections. The more information we can receive on why people kill and their motivations, the more informed our work can be. I'd really appreciate your help, darling." Joan smiled a nervous smile at me.

Her eyes were captivating. I straightened myself up on the couch and leaned forward toward Joan, getting uncomfortably close. I could see Marc squeezing Joan's hand as she sat back in reaction.

"A novel, erm? What about particularly?" I asked, intrigued.

To my dismay, Marc answered hastily.

"The madness of killers."

I paid no attention to his reply. I kept my eyes locked on Joan, even as she tried to look away, our eyes always met again. She smiled, her cheeks blushing.

"You are quite stunning, Mrs. Tracey. The most beautiful flower could not compete with your loveliness. Forgive me, but I seem to have become lost in your amber eyes."

Joan blushed. My eyes dropped to see her legs recrossing, lifting her face toward me. She pulled her hand from Marc's to mask her rosy cheeks.

"Mr. Lyle, please focus. We are here to discuss you. Mr. Tracey has posed a few questions, please humor him." Dr. Holmes understood what was happening.

"Mrs. Tracey, you must hear this often but have you considered films? Your beauty would shine on the big screen."

Her eyes light up in excitement, biting her lower lip. I leaned in a little closer, realizing I had her.

Marc reached for Joan's hand but she refused. She placed her hand atop her knee where her dress stopped. My eyes fixated to her legs as I knew she wanted. She was a natural tease. Dames like her basked in attention and glory. An endless hole needing, wanting to be filled with compliments and attention.

I tilted my head slightly toward Joan, cooing.

"Mmm. Absolutely stunning. You radiate Joan. You really do." I smiled a cool grin.

Marc stood up from the couch but Dr. Holmes intervened, pulling Marc to the side, leaving Joan and I alone for a moment. I reached in and watched as my hand met hers. She didn't object as I held her hand and lifted it to my face to lay a kiss. Her cheeks were red, her eyes were dilated, and I could feel her pulse from her wrist, her heart was racing. I asked her to lean in and began to mention sweet nothings in her ear as I caressed her hand. Her blushing was overtaken by her longing body. She melted into the seat beneath her, she was hot and bothered.

"I'm bewitched." I smiled at her.

Her giggle was interrupted by Dr. Holmes, who grabbed me by the collar of my shirt, lifting me to my feet.

"A word please, Mr. Lyle."

I raised my index finger at Joan and winked at her. She pulled her lips in to suppress her smile, coyishly giggling.

"In God's name, Mr. Lyle. You are trying to rile him up, aren't you?"

I refused to look at Dr. Holmes, instead, looking off into the distance at the statue of Buddha in the background corner.

"A religious man, are you, Dr. Holmes?"

I pointed to the statue and snickered. He turned to look at what I was pointing to then smacked my arm down.

"Now you listen here. Whatever you are planning, it ends, now. You may consider yourself an intelligent man, Mr. Lyle, but you are nothing more than a fool."

I dropped my eyes from the statue and immediately turned them onto Dr. Holmes, taking a step toward him. I exhaled a deep sigh. He looked down to see my clenched fists.

"Now, now. I think we have seen enough of you for tonight. I can have Richard escort you back to your room. Please wait here."

Dr. Holmes's raised hands dropped as he turned to walk to his phone. I motioned past him and walked directly up to Joan, whose eyes hadn't left my body, even as Marc desperately aimed for her attention.

"Joan, your interest in me, well, this place that surrounds us, is flattering. But, to get a real full picture for your studies, why don't you accompany the good doctor and myself into the actual asylum to get a *real* glimpse into true madness."

I turned my eyes and glared at Marc, then returned by gaze to Joan. Her face lit up in excitement, clapping her hands together.

"What a marvelous idea! I would so love this! Wouldn't we, Marc?"

Marc was staring at the ground, silent, but his frustration was audible with each groaning sigh. Joan nudged him after he fell silent.

"Isn't it a terrific idea, Marc? You are always saying how fascinating it would be to get *up close* and *personal.*"

She nudged Marc harder in the stomach.

"Erhm, yes, yes. Sure. If this is your wish, dear."

He remained looking at the ground, a defeated man. Dr. Holmes returned from the phone.

"Well Mr. Lyle, it was a pleasure having you, but it is time for you to return to your room as it is getting quite late. I'm sure the Tracey's are also ready to depart."

He opened his left arm to motion me to the exit but Joan interjected.

"On the contrary, Dr. Holmes. Lyle just mentioned a particularly interesting proposal. We would like to tour the asylum with Lyle, and you, of course."

Dr. Holmes broke out in a nervous laughter.

"What an interesting idea. Unfortunately, Mrs. Tracey, we cannot accommodate this request tonight. Both of your safety is paramount, and I would like to be able to plan for any necessities."

"Dr. Holmes, excuse me for questioning your ability, but you, yourself, have boasted of your control and innovative direction of this asylum since taking over from the wonderful Dr. Price. Is this only during particular moments or were you misleading?"

Joan's confidence glistened, attracting me to her more. I was captivated by this newfound resilience.

"Mrs. Tracey, I can assure you that this asylum is ran under my strict and professional guidance. A tight ship we have here."

His hands clamped behind his back revealed the frustration building in his bones.

"Well then, a man of your stature and nobility can accommodate your most ardent and affluent backers. My father, the Senator, of course, would be fascinated and relieved to know that his continual support of this institute is well-deserved."

I couldn't help but look down at the ground to hide my grin wiping across my face as Joan tore into Dr. Holmes.

What fun she must be.

A man as supercilious as him must feel impenetrable by any man and, accordingly, should by a woman.

"Joan, if the doctor feels it's not—"

Joan raised her hand up to Marc, cutting him off from his next words. This newfound Joan had never done this before, as Marc's expression was that of bewilderment.

"*I* would like to see the happenings behind these walls. Now, Dr. Holmes, please, lead the way."

Joan turned and waited for Dr. Holmes to respond with expectation. She was not to be haggled with. It was her way or else. And I ate it up.

"Mhmm."

I murmured under my breath.

"Don't worry, Doc, I'd be happy to walk with you through here."

I patted Dr. Holmes on the shoulder as he stood there, expressionless and disaffected. Joan laid a smile on me before turning back to Dr. Holmes.

"Well, Doctor?" She was insistent.

"Of course, Mrs. Tracey. I'd be happy to. Please wait here as I inform my top aid, Richard. One moment, please."

He turned his head down and angrily walked back to the back room, speaking indecipherable words under his breath.

"Good for you, Joan. That was marvelous. You *are* as remarkable and positively exquisite as I believed you to be."

I praised with a genuine smile.

She looked down to the ground shyly with a wide mouth grin, her confident demeanor vanishing under my stare. Dr. Holmes hastily returned with his hands still clenched behind his back.

"Well, it's been arranged. You all will follow me to the door ahead. Please take note to not stray from my side. This is not a place to engage in individual explorations. There is danger here, it is real, and it is without judgment. Understood? Now, please follow. I wouldn't want anyone to be hurt."

A slight shake of his head revealed his frustration as he made his way to the door. I beamed a laughing smiling toward Joan who reciprocated, then covering her mouth.

"Keep up, please. We enter through here."

Dick opened the door, motioning for us to enter. I looked to Marc to see his dismayed and beaten face. Joan elated in excitement, and Dr. Holmes simmered in frustration. I, myself, beamed with joy. This shall be fun.

CHAPTER TWENTY-TWO

AS WE WALKED THROUGH THE door into the frozen hell, the reminder of this place encroached on my spirit. Joan's face immediately shifted, the smile fading. The quick realization of where she was, where we all were, quickly encroached.

"Erhm, what an interesting place this already seems to be." Joan looked back at me for reassurance. I motioned for her to continue forward.

Straightaway the chamber-like hallways and sparse glimpses of light reveled in the torturous frigid airs. Marc's leather shoes squeaked with every step he took down the hallway, splashing into the puddles of water falling from the pipes above. The squeaking infuriated me more with each step. Before I could make mention of this irritability, Dr. Holmes reached out his right arm to stop us. I turned back to see Dick following behind me. I hadn't noticed the truncheon gripped tightly in his left hand.

Dick pushed at my left shoulder, ensuring my eyes met his.

"Whatever happens, this is on yer ass," he whispered.

Dick lifted the truncheon to eye level. I could see the scuffs littered throughout. I half-smirked at him before turning back around to face Dr. Holmes.

"Ah. Everything *seems* fine. Let's continue."

The lines on Dr. Holmes's forehead filled his face as worry enveloped him.

The flickering lights in the next passing hallway added to the tension. It was palpable. As we ascended downward, my breath became increasingly visible. Joan rubbed her arms in an attempt to mask her shaking. Marc's attention fell from Joan to the floor, carefully examining each step, awaiting what *could* be.

We were all unsure of what we were walking into, but the aura was unnatural. There was *something* thick in the air. The moment was ripe with fear and hesitation. We pressed forward, coming upon several rooms paralleling the hallway. I was intrigued to see a window allowing access through the metal door.

Dr. Holmes lifted the light to the end of the hall, inching toward it slowly. He leerily turned his head back, displaying an uneasiness I was unaccustomed to seeing from him. Joan had fallen back from Marc as if she was unsure if she wanted to continue.

I leaned toward her and whispered, "Spooked, are we?"

Joan's shoulders raised as she tried to hide her panic.

"No, no, not at all, Mr. Lyle. It's just . . . different than how I imagined it to be. All the tales Dr. Holmes had told, well—I guess they really are just that. I'm not so certain I should be down here anymore. I was a little hast—"

"Darling, do not underestimate yourself. I know you can do this. Fearless, brave beauty that you are. This is for your research, is it not? Now imagine regaling your peers with tales and spectacles of your time here in a real asylum. The journey, the prize! The grandiosity! You'll be an international hit!"

Despite her reluctance, I knew this broad longed for fame outside of daddy's shadow. Her identity dwelled on being the "Senator's daughter," but she craved something more. This is what attracts me to her. Her desire. It seemed insatiable. I could see the wheels turning in her eyes as I spoke. The unquenchable taste of fame is interminable. She *needs* this.

"This can be dangerous, no?"

"Oh dear, was I wrong about you? I pegged you for a dame unlike others. One longing for more." I reached for her hand, rubbing it between my palms. "Was I mistaken? I surely hope not." I lifted her hand and planted a soft peck.

Her body squirmed, naturally falling closer to mine.

"Well no . . ."

A smile lifted her worried face, her eyebrows relaxing.

"I'm just acting silly. I'm sure there is nothing to be so worried about."

She bit her lip and brushed my shoulder, eyeing me before I turned her around to hurry us back to the group.

Marc had also pushed forward, forgetting to look back for Joan, concentrating on each step. His hands were balled in tight fists, seemingly to hide the shaking of his body.

As we reached Dr. Holmes, Marc turned to see Joan and I together. The expression of fear fell to jealousy. He grabbed her by the arm and pulled her into him, shoving me into the concrete wall. Realizing what he had done, his eyes widened and his mouth attempted to quiver an apology. I enjoyed this feistiness. I grinned at Marc before lifting my hands in surrender. I motioned for them to move forward together as I turned back to see if Dick was following, but the darkness engulfed my vision.

What happened to the faint lights?

I stood there, puzzled. The hallway, the area, *were different.* Unexplainable. A breeze brushed my shoulder. Wherever Dick was, the immersion of darkness fell upon him.

A faint shadow of what I hoped was Marc or Joan guided me as I hastily moved to catch up with them. But the darkness glided over the walls, pulling the light further and further away. The cold whip of wind danced on my neck, pushing me to quicken my pace.

They can't be that far ahead. I'm damn near running.

I broke out into a sprint watching as the darkness raced me through the maze-ways.

Nothing is making sense.

My breath was audible and my heart pumped for more air. It has been some time since I had last run. The oversized boots quickly became a nuisance to my feet. The rubbing against the grain was starting to form blisters.

I reached my hands out to watch for the walls. I was near pure darkness. I slowed my pace, nearing a complete stop. I felt myself turning in circles, it all looked the same. I was unsure of where I was.

How could this be?

My chest pounded in my throat as I lifted my hands to my head to catch my breath.

What is this Godforsaken place? I was right behind them! How is this so?

My hands clenched behind my head in both fear and anger. I reached back to feel for the wall to rest, hoping to quiet my breath to listen, to listen for them, for anything. Any slight sense of sound. Silence ballooned.

I stood there, motionless. Although I was immersed in darkness, my head felt as if it was spinning. I needed to center myself. But the farther I felt my hand reach back expecting a wall, the closer the empty feeling of air came. I pulled my hands back to my face, rubbing viciously at me eyes.

No wall? What the hell? There has to be a wa—I'm just tired, that's it. Just need to take a deeper breath, slow my heart.

I grabbed my knees and hesitantly reached farther down, relieved to find the concrete floor. Sighing in relief, I stood up, unsure of which direction I had come or was going. The room was still spinning, taking hold of me. My stomach churned, roaring in anger. I reached for my stomach but my body collapsed to the floor.

My breath slowed to sluggish exhales but my heart was racing in anticipation. I covered my mouth to listen. The eerie silence echoed through this hallway or wherever I was. A striking pain bulged on my left foot. I reached down to touch for the shoe. I found the lacing and pulled the shoe off, feeling under the foot. A warm liquid hugged my fingers.

Damn it! Fuck!

I squeezed my foot in frustration. The striking pain was rivaling the tumbling of my stomach and the spinning of my head. I closed my eyes and slammed my fists against the concrete floor.

"Fuck!" I screamed.

As soon as the words left my mouth, a piercing noise, *the* noise struck my ears. The floor below me gave way and I felt myself falling backward. A flood of light flashed forcefully to my eyes, nearly blinding me. I rushed to cover but my head was whipped back, sending me into unconsciousness.

"Mr. Lyle. Mr. Lyle. Can you hear me? Can you hear me?"

I felt a pull on my wrists, a tightening. My ankles strained.

"James Lyle, sit up!"

The sensation of water dripped down my face, waking me. I tried to lift my arms to rub at my blurry eyes but felt them confined. I pulled again.

What the hell? I'm strapped?

"Now the chest, Ron. Make sure he's cinched in tight."

"Where's the sponge?"

"I need more saline, it wasn't wet enough."

"You don't want it too wet otherwise it'll short circuit! Dammit, get to it! We haven't all day!"

My eyes could only see silhouettes of men walking around me, clouded by a haze. The voices were clear and distinct but foreign. I attempted to speak, to ask where I was but felt a tightening around my chest. In the haze, I could see a faint brown around my waist. My head was forcibly lifted, feeling more liquid spill down my face.

"Attach the skullcap then blindfold him, hurry up now!"

My vision cleared, showing where I was. I froze. I could see several men gawking. All unfamiliar faces, eager in excitement. Except for one. The man dressed in a dated suit. He stood there, peering down at his watch in annoyance, then dropping his hands to his waist. But something moved to my line of sight, shifting out of the shadow of the men. The unmistakable eyes pierced through. The men fell into shadows as the light above me blurred my line of sight.

My body motioned to stand but was quickly forced down by the straps confining me. I was locked in.

"Are we ready?"

"Just about! This damn cap, it always gives me trouble! Warden, we need to get someone to look at it. It gave me trouble with the—"

The man in the dated suit barked, "Just hurry, damn it! I have a golf lunch with the governor and this is bleeding into my time!"

No! No! No! No! This, this, NO! I CAN'T BE HERE! NO!

"Just about—Got it! Okay."

The man stood back, admiring me as a canvas, throwing his hands together in excitement.

"We are a go!"

The trembling of my body shifted the leather straps against the grain of the wood in the chair. The eyes were locked in on me. They had not wavered, had not blinked. They were there.

"What boy, are you afraid now?"

A guard mockingly laughed, mimicking a crying face.

My legs quivered, my heart beating against my ribcage. I grabbed at the chair, digging my nails in, splinters rushed into my fingers but I dug in deeper. My mouth fell open but words never formed. Words had escaped me. Lost in the fear of what was happening. My mind raced with the thought of my imminent death.

A fatter guard bent at his waist to ogle.

"Oh, don't be scared, boyo. You had to know this was coming. Hell awaits!"

He snickered, placing his hands in his pockets, turning away. But just behind him stood the entity. Grinning from ear to ear. That sickening distorted smile.

"NOW!"

I braced, gritting my teeth and squeezed my eyes closed. The echoes of my screams jolted my ears.

My eyes shot open to reveal Dr. Holmes leaning over me.

"Marvelous!"

CHAPTER TWENTY-THREE

"NOW, MR. LYLE, YOU MAY experience a few oddities. Do not worry, it is all for the better! Breathtaking, isn't it?"

I attempted to sit up but the throbbing of my head and nausea pitted in my stomach pressed me back against the table. I clenched at my forehead, a headache raging inward.

"Now, let me check your teeth, I'm going to remove the cloth. Let's see now, open wide. Ah yes, perfect, not a shattered tooth in sight! Now, to check your extremities, you had a rather unexpectedly violent series of quakes. I'm going to lift your legs and your arms. Please let me know if anything feels a miss."

He lifted and bended each leg and arm. But the pounding of my head was all I could think of.

"No sight of a fracture or a broken bone in sight, splendid! Absolutely splendid! I couldn't be any more pleased."

He brought his palms together as a smile gleamed on his face.

"What . . ." was all I could mutter. The pain overtaking my words.

"Experimentation is science, my dear. It's Metrazol."

He leaned in, his breath blowing on my cheeks. My body lay immobile, but my eyes met his.

"The pain should only be temporary, but it shall be a few days before we can see the after effects. Be patient, we may have to do this many times, among other things. You have become quite ill, Mr. Lyle."

I turned my eyes away from the giddy smile, looking to the light hanging above. The pounding nearly reaching its breaking point.

"Come, come, now." Dr. Holmes brushed the hair off the top of my forehead, pulling my face to meet his. "This is never easy. But, I can assure you, it shall work."

He stood up and called for a cold washcloth.

"Here, let's place this on. That'll do it. Ah, better already?"

He laid the cloth on my forehead, then walked away.

The coolness of the cloth was a relief to my heated forehead. My body drew from the cold, sucking it in. I closed my eyes and leaned back against the table, yearning for a reprieve. A sudden wretched feeling in my stomach climbed up out of my throat, I leaned over and spewed out. The ferocity of the vomiting dropped me to the floor, catching on my stomach. My cheek met the cold concrete flooring, waking me for just a moment before my eyes finally rolled back.

"Lyle! Lyle! You okay there?"

I felt a nudge to my shoulder, waking me.

"Lyle, come on now? Say something there mate!"

My eyes fought to stay closed, heavy as they were. I slowly lifted my hand to my face, rubbing my palm into my left eye as my right cheek still laid in a cold liquid.

I mustered a groan, still unable to speak a semblance of words.

"You look like hell, chap."

The voice became clear with each passing second. It's familiarity warmed me. That damn accent. That bloody annoying accent. *Tommy*?

"T . . . t . . . t-tommy?"

After multiple attempts, I was finally able to push my body over onto my back. The lights casted down hellacious rays of shine. Slowly, I was able to lift my hands to shield my face from the exposure. Tommy's face blurred into view.

"Yeah mate, who else would it be?"

He chuckled. His sense of humor threw me. I haven't seen him in such a time. By now, I couldn't even say when. Hours, days, weeks, maybe months? Time has warped. Everything feels as if it's an illusion. I cannot be sure that this is even real. I wanted to reach out, to feel if he was actually there, but my body lay weak pressing against the cold concrete floor. I squinted my eyes to verify Tommy's presence.

"How are you . . . here?"

"Whaddya mean? You must be utterly knackered. I'd help you up if I could, but this chair kind of prevents it a bit, don't ya say?"

He lifted his right arm to showcase his chair. A feeling of disbelief was quashed with his sly humorous bits. That was Tommy. In all the nights we had spent speaking through the walls, I could always count on him for a good laugh. We'd spend hours laughing, speaking, regaling about the past, his time in America, my time in New York. He had come from a similar home back in his own country. His father was a coal miner as well before the coal dust got to him. His "mum" and sister gathered Tommy at age thirteen and brought him to America, after his father died, to stay with his grandparents who had relocated to New York.

I always wondered how he was able to hold his sense of humor through it all. I turned vengeful, full of disdain toward the world, but he saw humor in every bit of the world, even offering kindness when it wasn't deserved. With me. I felt hopeless, broken, but he offered me a piece of humanity I forgot could exist.

His circumstances, bound to a chair for the rest of his life, would have crushed any other man, but he never relented. But Tommy wasn't always that way. His love for running and walking the streets at night had helped him to meet various types of people in this new country, for better or worse. But more than anything, he simply wanted to fit in. New York's mean streets don't offer kindness, instead they come with judgment and harshness; he was sure to stand out.

"You are a cheeky little fella there, aren't ya?"

My attempt at humor got to him. A smile burst onto his face, his features growing into focus. His hazel eyes rained a calamity I hadn't experienced in some time, but the dimples on his face always managed to crack any sense of frustration I might have had. His smile lit up his entire face, becoming contagious to even the sharpest jaw. He looked better than I had last seen him. Calm. Cool. Happy. It was . . . odd.

"Now yer gettin' it! Gonna teach ya proper humor if it kills me! Now, let's get ya up from down there."

His sun-streaked locks of hair ran into his forehead, causing him to push it back with his left hand as he flashed another smile at me before reaching out his right hand.

"Come on now. Phew, mate. You smell wretched down there."

Reaching for his hand, I drunkenly stood, uneasy, attempting to gather myself. The blaring lights above seem to be drawing painfully near.

"Ah, come, come, I'm funny. A regular Chaplin here."

I joked.

"But Tommy, what's with the bright lights there? Are you trying blind me? What gives?"

"Ah, those, that's not of my doing there, mate. That's the good Doc. Sick bastard he is. Enjoys his futile mind games and torturous equipment. But is it getting to ya? A little light throwing you off now, is it? The big, bad Lyle perturbed by some bright lights. That'll kill yer legend. Ha. Don't tell that to the papers, we'll keep that a secret between us."

"Just a little much for my skin now; have to keep this dashing face protected from harmful rays such as these. Could blind a person. Now, I need to get this vomit off of me before it ruins my mystique as well, don't you say?"

We both cackled as I tried to wipe off the dried crust from my lips.

"Yeah, yer looking great with all that on ya. A real statement now. Ya traded in tailor suits for shabby clothes, frazzled hair, and bile. Absolutely incredible!"

He smacked his knee jeering in pride at his rhetoric.

"It's, it's really great to see you," I said. "Last time I had seen you, you seemed lost, out of it. Unlike yourself. With Lockeheart then your visit with Dr. Psycho, it just didn't seem right."

"None of it is. Or will be. Not until we are out. Damn lunatics running this place. The Doc himself, Holmes, he's a real piece of work there. Calls all of this experiments. More like torture it is. Just like a proper posh, using the poor and unworthy to test out. That madman threw me into a tub of ice for hours last time! If my legs could feel, I'm sure they were frozen!" He smirked.

"You're the madman, Tommy!" I laughed. "You'd think Englishman to Englishman, he'd have some pity?"

"He's no Englishman. The man's a devil. Pure and simple maniacal demon. Proper evil."

"What he has been doing, in these experiments, treatments, any of it, I can't seem to make out what's real or not anymore. Tommy, my mind, it feels as if it's tearing itself apart. I'm out there, then in the hallway, now I'm in here with you. Say, how did you get down here anyway. How'd you manage that? Got an in with the good doctor now?"

"Yes, certainly, we are *pals* now. The best of friends! Are you out of yer Goddamn mind? Well, ya are, but even more so? No, there has been some concern with ya lately. Lyle, you've been . . . different. A little out of yer head a bit, mate."

His words dropped a weight on me. I wasn't sure what to make of his words. His tone deepened and his eyes widened. The banter of Tommy Lancaster vanished as he donned a doomed concerned look. His eyes drifted to the floor and his hands folded atop his legs.

"I . . . I don't seem to be understanding . . ."

"Y'er screams. At night. They're chilling. Worse than before. It doesn't sound like ya, not even in the slightest. I'm concerned, I really am. I try to talk to you through the walls, like we used to, ya know? But you aren't answering anymore. But I still hear you talking. Talking as if someone is in the room with ya. It's a wee bit creepy there, mate. I just needed to know that you were fine. I made quite the fuss until I was able to visit—"

I cut him off, what he was saying didn't seem to make sense. Screaming at night? Talking to myself? How could he hear any of this? He was moved, there wasn't anyone in the room near me, I passed them, they were empty. He had to be mistaken.

"Tommy, what you are saying, all of it, it just doesn't add up. You were moved, look, there's, you seem to be mistaken. But we need to leave here, this place, there is something wrong with it. We need to plan an escape and go now, another minute here and we—"

My mouth continued to move but a white silence deepened in my head, ringing to my ears. The brightness of the room struck me. My neck muscles tightened.

"My head, my head . . ." was all I could hear myself whispering reluctantly.

A squeezing pressure perturbed my forehead. I buried my face in my palms hoping to dispel the brightness of the malicious lighting up above, but it peered through the open crevices between my fingers.

I could physically feel the radiating light bearing down into my skin, burning it. Sweltering heat beckoned from my neck. I could almost smell the burning hairs. I squeezed my eyes shut, collapsing to the floor, my energy sucked dry.

A distant and far cry of my name echoed slightly outweighed only by the fury of the brightness building upon me. My forearm hit my forehead. I could feel a fever breaking out as sweat dripped to cool my overheated body. The room's temperature increased drastically. I felt as if I was turning over a fire, cooking internally and rapidly.

I opened my eyes to pull my shirt over my face but saw footsteps scrambling on the floor. I could see the drops of sweat forming puddles around me. I frantically reached down for my shirt but felt the break of a cool hand clutched at my wrist, pulling it over my face, exposing me to the light. The pain blistered over my face, shooting up from my legs to the top of my head like fire. I was reeling in agony. My other wrist was yanked.

"Grab him! Grab him down, damn it! Hold on to him!"

Waterfalls of liquid bled down my face. I was unsure if it was still sweat.

"Disrobe him, hurry up! But don't let go! Damnit, I said not to let go!"

The voices blended with the light above, unable to discern who or what was happening around me.

"Strap him down, quickly! He's—"

The vomit pouring down my neck likened to lava seeping through my flesh. My inaudible screams should have punctured the blood vessels in my forehead.

Dear God. Help me! I can't, I can't go on anymore! I can't!

I squeezed my eyes shut with a desperate prayer to a God I wasn't sure I believed in.

If this was hell, it was worse than I had anticipated. But if, if this wasn't, my soul would forever be ensnared in this tormented pasture. The devil has had more than his indulgences.

I would've prayed to anyone, for any reprieve, to be anywhere. The electric chair seemed to be a benevolent option. A firing squad, anything but *this*.

"Hold him still! Useless you all are! Hold him now, I need to administer this before he breaks!"

A sharp pinch in my stomach followed a wave of welcomed darkness rushing over my eyes. My shoulders fell, allowing my head to relax. Drips of water splashed down on my chin, pleasuring my inflamed skin. I opened my eyes to see the faint light flickering above me. I quickly sat up.

How? How am I back here? What is this Godforsaken place.

I was back in the hallway, alone, and nearly disrobed.

CHAPTER TWENTY-FOUR

I LIFTED MY ARMS TO the faint light and brought my knees to my stomach.

No burns? No burns.

I was relieved to see my skin undisturbed but the lack of clothing was concerning. Is this part of some sick game? Was I drugged?

The wine. There must have been, had to have been something in there.

Dr. Holmes, Dick, Marc, and . . . Joan, they all, all had to be in on this. The tingling in my toes suggested I may have been asleep longer than I had imagined. I shook at my feet, wanting to wake them before I stood. The water continued to slide down my back from the pipes above, a contrast to the sweltering heat. It's drop felt heavy, unwanted; my skin felt sensitive to the touch, tender in its recovery.

Was this a dream? A nightmare? *But Tommy.* Was he a dream? Is he even alive? Have I slumped into the circles of hell with the Devil gleefully playing tricks on my mind? How am I to discern between reality and what isn't anymore? Pain is no longer a reliable factor; it is felt in the dream state and in whatever reality I seem to be in.

As baffled as I was, I needed to move quickly from the dripping. I stomped my feet against the floor to wake them, then planted them, readying myself. I tensed my muscles and lifted one knee up at a time. The drips painfully continued, reminding me to hurry. I finally stood, wavering in my steps and dizzy, but I was comforted to finally feel the wall beside me.

Where has this been?

I leaned against it for assistance, stumbling slowly down the corridor.

The frigid airs numbed the aches pulsating from my body. As cold as it was, my body desperately needed the relief from whatever I had experienced in my dream state. My feet led my mind, pleading with the floor for a pathway out of this nightmare. My pace sluggishly quickened.

The halls seemed endless but mundane and consistent; I was unable to differentiate between them. It all looked as one. The concrete color bled from floor to top. The weathered building's age showed with each cobweb fixated in the corners and rats desperately running through the halls. I had no sense of direction or an end goal. I just needed to leave. A feeling of dread and worry belted me. I needed to escape, not only this hallway but this wretched place. I wasn't sure if I was running away from something or to, but everything inside me signaled that my time here needed to end.

The dread pressed in harder, pushing my tired legs to quicken their pace. My body was torn, exhausted, riddled in pain, but anxious to make my way out at any costs. I visualized the exit and kept pushing forward, reminding myself that I may not make another hour or day here. These people here, Dr. Holmes, all of them, this was not a reformatory but a living hell. And I have had enough.

But I was suddenly drawn to a halt as I came across a lone room in the next hallway. The thick metal door was wide open, inviting me in. A strong desire lit inside of me. I wanted to enter this room. I needed to. And I wasn't sure why that had to be. It was calling out to me, to my body. I turned my feet toward the open door as the darkness summoned me. My mind was unrelenting in its warnings. Every sense of danger ripened with each step. But I felt a pulling, a yearning inside me, but it wasn't of me.

My feet, reminded of the repeated warnings emanating from my head, carefully measured each step forward. As I drew near, a fetid smell blew toward my nostrils but I didn't react. I couldn't. I was no longer in control;

a force was beckoning me forward. The room had seemed near but each step felt like hours away and I was thankful for this. The newly christened crinkles on my forehead lifted with my eyebrows as I braced for what I would see.

I took another step forward, coming to the entrance of the room, stopping just before I could enter. My mind was screaming to not enter through. Before my feet were able to take another step, my arms lifted in the air to block myself from pushing forward. My body was conflicted, wanting, needing to enter, but my mind had unknown reservations. The warnings were unclear but deepened with each passing second. A sense that if I entered, I may never come back ran through me. A chill lifted the hairs on the back of my neck.

I dropped my head, my hands still pushing against the walls, blocking my entrance. But a sweet drift blew to my face replacing the rancid swell drifting through the hallway. It was intoxicating. I took a deep inhale, wanting to soak it all in, to feel it in every part of my skin, deep within my bones. The desire intensified, voraciously, nearing out of control. It was insatiable. My first hit of the drug again. It was addicting. I needed more.

My hands fell immediately to my side. The eagerness of my feet stepped forward into the darkness as all worry was washed away. I stepped into the obscurity. inhaling the euphoria. The door slammed behind me but I didn't care. The sensation dug deeper into my body. My mouth fell open and my eyes rolled back in pleasure.

CHAPTER TWENTY-FIVE

I STEPPED INTO A ROOM enclosed by darkness. I could not see before me nor behind. Whether my eyes were open or shut was debatable. My quick breaths were building like a symphony near its crescendo. I was quickly reminded of the bareness of my body as the stifling temperatures engulfed the room. That glorious feeling quickly dissipated as my body stiffened, needing another hit of it.

What am I doing in here?

I hastily turned my body and dashed for where I had entered, frantically searching for the door lever to escape.

Where is it? Where is this fucking lever? Goddamn it!

I kicked and punched at the door, desperate to make my escape, my mind's warnings shouting of the danger yet to come.

My battered hands continued to press into the wall but it quickly turned to horror as I could not find an exit. My flailing sounds in the dark were quickly silenced by a long drawn creek deepening from behind me. My heart near leapt out of my chest at the sound. My eyes squeezed shut, fearing what that might be.

I mustn't see it. I can't see it. I will not.

But my eyes shot open to a tapping on my left shoulder. My heart nearly gave out with my body freezing in place. But what stood before me was not what I was expecting. The room was visible, unlike any I had seen here. An unknown light illuminated the plastered red striped wallpaper bleeding from the surrounding walls. A door had seeped behind the wallpaper, becoming invisible in my line of sight. There was no exit forward. I had to turn around and face what was behind me. Whatever had tapped my shoulder, the thought of someone, something else in here with me, had a thousand thoughts racing through my mind.

Am I to die here, now? Is this my end?

Gritting my teeth, I ran over my options, but they all lead to one: turning around. There was no way out before me, if I had any chance, it was behind me.

Whatever, whoever, they could have killed me by now, but they haven't.

I held my breath to listen behind me. The creaking noise had ceased and the freezing temperatures were now bearable. My heart's rapid beating in my ears was all I could hear. But a second tapping, a more aggressive one, had me trembling as my leg muscles tightened, causing a prominent pain in my calves. In my peripherals, I was unable to catch wind of a figure.

I balled my fists and swiftly turned around, readying my stance for what I would face.

Nothing.

My shoulders fell, relaxing as I unclenched my fist. I let out a deep sigh as I had been holding my breath for some time. The rooms atmosphere lifted, from complete terror to a more comfortable feeling of unknown. My hands lifted, feeling my chest. I was still alive. I looked up, was this God's doing or the Devil?

But a feeling of celebration fell as my eyes returned to what was before me. My eyes wandered to the opened wooden door some steps before me.

Is this some kind of trap? The tapping, is that where it exited? There's no other way out. Fuck!

I bent down to grab at my knees but my eyes remained locked on the door, unsure if something were to pop out unexpectedly.

Quickly glancing around the room for any other possible exits, I returned my stare to the door. There was no other way out. Taking a deep inhale, hands placed firmly on my knees, I wondered what awaited, or who?

Can I do this? Can I fucking do this? Am I even me anymore? Who am I? Is this real?

Lifting from my knees, I stood upright, shoulders pushed back, glaring at the door. But in my sideline, I noticed an inauspicious change in the room.

Were the walls always this close? The wallpaper, why can I see it fully from the corner of my eyes? Jesus, it's moving closer. The Goddamn room is closing in on me.

As I had stood there, lost in my thoughts, I failed to notice the room trying to box me in. I reached out my hands, flabbergasted that I could nearly feel all four sides of the room with a simple stretch of my arms.

My thoughts raced, fighting against this reality. My body started to feel the wallpaper closing in on me. My breaths shallowed as I knew I needed to make a decision or face a crushing death.

Fuck!

Frantic, I ran forward toward the door, leaving behind the trapping red wallpaper.

Made it, Goddamn, that was close.

Closing the door behind me, I was relieved I had avoided the chambers of hell and had re-entered the hallway. The familiar color of the concrete walls were a welcoming sight to my anxious body. But I did not let my guard down. And I was right not to. The hallway was not as I had left it. I lifted my hand to my face in disbelief.

This fucking place!

I must've fallen into the depths of hell, tortured to wander here, lost forever. There is no other explanation. The hallway had inverted. I stepped back, leaning against the wall, grabbing at my hair, leaning down into my legs. I was sure I had shattered my vocal cords as my screams roared in frustration and fear.

Rising back up, I disgustingly looked at the endless hallway before me. Slamming my palms against the wall, I took a step forward, ready to take on whatever madness this evil had left. Creaks of doors opening stopped me in my tracks. I watched several doors on opposite ends of the hallway open on their own. These were not the same heavy doors I had become accustomed to in the asylum, these were similar to the wooden door in the red room. All had creaked open in unison, creating a disturbing groaning that echoed together

I turned to look back but met face-to-face with an concrete wall. Furiously, I ran my fists against the wall, breaking skin as all the anger and frustration was mounting in ways I could no longer contain. Warm drips of blood painted my throbbing knuckles. I wanted to belt out another scream but my aching throat refused to let out another sound. My hands at my side, feeling the crimson trailing down my fingers to the ground beneath me, I waited. Time was standing still in this inverted hell. Picking my hand up to the wall, I leaned up against it, my mind exhausted and my spirit crushing.

There is no way out of here.

My mind raced with existential thoughts of roaming these endless and nonsensical halls until I entered into madness. I could see myself, withering away, starved, yearning for more than thirst, for clarity. I yearn for it now.

Pull yourself together. Come on, come on. Pull your damn self together.

My mind was not ready to give up. I was not ready to give in. Turning from the wall, I faced the opened doors, unsure of what may thwart my next stops. But I waited. Standing there, motionless, leaning back against the wall, staring ahead, jaw clenched. My mind went blank, my ears closed, and my eyes blurred. My eyes were entranced, lost in the endless sea of unknown in front of me.

But there was no other way out, no other way in. *This*, this was the only way forward. Or backward. Staying trapped here will do no good other than aiding in the loss of my sanity. Snapping back into reality I shook my head, awaking my eyes and quelling the trance-like state. Taking a deep inhale, I slowly stepped forward, tightening my fists, ready to strike at whatever may surprise.

Each step I took felt even further away than I had before. The doors seemed farther than I had initially imagined, but I continued in my journey, anxious to leave this hallway at all costs.

As I neared the first door, I heard a faint voice growing in intensity as I approached. The words were not audible, but the tone was stern, riddled with anger, and threatening. I wasn't sure if I wanted to approach a situation such as this, so I quieted my steps, listening, needing to hear more.

Slowly and quietly, I tried to calm my breathing as I was sure my thumping heart rate would give me away. Wringing my hands and fingers by my side, I stilled my body against the concrete just outside of the first door. All sounds had ceased. An uncomfortable silence filled the air. Closing my eyes, I readied myself to peer into the room, nervous and terrified of who or what I would see. I prepared myself, closing my fists tightly against my sides, clenching down on my teeth. One last inhale was taken before I peered my head over to the opening of the door, looking inside. My eyes exploded open, my jaw falling open, I was taken back.

Crouching desperately in the corner, tears streaming down his face, pleading, begging for mercy, was a man I had recognized from so long ago. He had his hands wrapped around his bare legs, he was nearly undressed, wearing only his undergarments, eyes shut, afraid to look up.

No, no, this, this isn't real. This cannot be happening.

Rubbing furiously at my eyes, I tried to wake myself. Opening my eyes, I was no longer at the helm of the door; instead, I was towering above the man. Towering above Andrew with a 357 Magnum resting on his forehead. He opened his glassy eyes, begging one more time for mercy before I felt my hand jerk back. His head thwarted back, hitting the tile below. The gun fell from my hands, catching a glimpse of the blood splatter on my hand.

This moment felt different. It wasn't as it had felt before, euphoric and unyielding. Instead, an inchoate mixture of tragedy and desolation flowed through my bones. It was crushing. The weight, the gravity of it, was immense. Andrew was forsaken. As he deserved, but I needed deliverance. Dropping the gun, I desperately pleaded with my feet to run out of the room. Luckily, they obliged. As I took my last step out of that room, I turned my head to face it, glancing at Andrew's body as the door creaked slowly shut on its own.

Turning forward, I stared at the remaining doors before me. Fourteen of them I counted. Fourteen for the men I had killed. In counting them, I had noticed some had closed, as I had relived them before. But the final door, it was firmly shut. My apparent exit. The only way out of this hallway. It loomed over the others as the largest door, different in its size and color. Not composed of wood as had the others but a boastful gold-plated exterior. Staring at it for some time, a tear developed in my eye, wavering above my cheek before finally falling. I firmly knew what was in there. What I would see. What I would feel. That door I had no desire to enter. That door would undoubtedly be the most difficult. My final kill. The most painful. But the most necessary.

CHAPTER TWENTY-SIX

A FAINT VOICE INSIDE ME knew I had to enter into each one of these open doors to exit. There was no other way out. I would have to play this game, reliving every single kill, every single memory, but condemned to having the pleasure, the joy stripped from my senses. Each door was a stark reminder of who I was. Who I still am. Every name was ingrained in my soul. And now, in these rooms. There was no escaping them. The faces, their glossy tear-filled eyes. Each one grew into me, a part of my being, my existence. I could not dream without the sounds of their screams echoing in untold creatures and features. I killed them but they were reborn inside of me. Very much alive and feeding upon my inner masochistic desires.

I needed to kill. Just as I needed to breathe, the urge to kill was insatiable, unapologetic, and lustful. My first kill was done out of necessity, a fight for survival. But the feelings, the joy that followed after, it was a drug I had to chase as it could not be quenched elsewhere. The desire grew ravenously after each one. A revolver, a knife, a rope, whatever means of opportunity was presented, I gleefully executed.

But these men, these were not men of opportunity. These were calculated attacks on greed, lust, and evil. The lives they had chosen brought them to me. My desires beckoned for their sacrifices. Men of corruption, of scandal, of torturous rule over the vulnerable. These were the men I watched, waited, then claimed my stake. Men of higher power who were tainting the world around them. Tainting my world. I needed hope that good existed here, and they were in the way.

It helped that I knew these men: acquaintances some, others Charles managed their money or had run into from time to time. Watching all these high rise men wither to their knees, the gleeful smiles sour to cries of agony or desperation, pleading for their lives opened a space in my heart I had not known was void. Their screams emptied into that space, filling it every time. I remember, after each had taken their final breath, lighting a cigarette, basking in the moment, peering down at the life fading from their veins and into mine. There is not a drug in the world that can replicate that pure emotion.

After entering nine doors and witnessing the multiple murders, the staged hangings, and the blood splatter, my body, my mind, it had enough. I exited the ninth room listening to the repetitive creek of the door closing behind me but was alarmed to see a different door open before me. I froze in my tracks, counting the doors repeatedly, praying to count a total of fourteen. But every time I would end with the same number.

Fifteen.

Fifteen? How is that possible? I know every man I killed. There must be some mistake; there has to be. This, this is all a dream anyway. My imagination, naturally, running wild. That's it. Or maybe I'm double counting a room.

But there was no denying the black door in front of me. I could not see within as it was captured in darkness. I turned to face the other doors, but they firmly shut as I stared. There was no way around, I had to enter.

An uneasiness crowded the space between the entrance and my body. But I had made it so far, there was no other escape. I lifted my hands from my sides in front of me, readying my body for the darkness. The steps echoed a loudness I was suspicious of as the light lifted and I was submerged in darkness. The door behind me hastily shut, locking me in.

My inhalations were noisy, pushing out through my nostrils, fighting against an uneasiness; my eyes looking to adjust. Motioning around the room, I tried to feel for a wall or anything to provide a center. An abrupt and stinging sensation lingered on the base of my spine. I yelped in agony as another blow quickly struck again. Furiously, I turned my body, fighting the pain, to face what was happening. Before me, I was met with these dead yellowed eyes that struck terror into my soul.

The ambience of the room melted in a fury of internal dread and horror. The pungent smell of sulfur littered the room. The descents of hell had made its way to me. I could no longer feel the beating of my heart against my chest as my lungs fought for air, holding my breath unknowingly. My eyes were locked on the sight before me. If the room had lifted from its darkness, I wouldn't have noticed.

The eyes lured me into the depths of a hell I had never experienced. All thoughts dissipated and all energy evaporated.

Trying to pull myself from its weighted stare, my mind tried to make sense of what was before me. My eyes bled into the creature, digging for a visualization, but no image remained. It was morphing rapidly in front of me. No still sight could be contained. It was purposeful and deliberate.

My clammy hands and antsy feet reflected a fear building deep within my bones. My darkest nightmares could not draw up the visual I was trying to perceive.

Another furious blow from behind knocked me to the ground. Glimpses of light flickered throughout the room coming in bits to my foggy head. Attempting to situate myself up from the floor, my hands dug into a cool dirt floor. My eyes fell to the floor, examining the sudden change. The walls had melted into a familiar wood look, giving me pause and a tug in the pits of my stomach.

"Get up, boy! C'mon now, ya girly boy! I'll make a man out of ya now! Get up!"

Jim's voice shook my senses as it dripped from his tone descending into another, more sinister, malevolent voice. My nails dug deeper into the dirt. The welt from my spine blistered voraciously. I turned my head to see a ghost of Jim's image *and* the creature manifesting into one, approaching near.

On my hands and knees, I exhaled a hard breath, embracing for another blow that never came. My mind twirled between horror and anger, signaling to my body to quickly stand. Slowly lifting my left leg up, I caught my breath, the blistering pain striking. I exhaled a harder breath and stood fully up, facing open air.

I turned my head from left to right, searching for a sight, only catching glimpses of a decayed and decrepit version of the house I grew up in. The smell of sulfur had vanished, but a gust of heat slapped across my face. I dropped my hands to my knees, looking to catch my breath, but the pain was engulfing my senses.

"Think I left, didn't ya? Think y'er so tough. Y'er not shit, boy, never have, never will be. Do ya hear me, boy? Do ya?"

Jim lifted his arm to whip another lash across my back, but it was caught by an unexpectedly furious blow from my right hand. Then a left. Blows piled on until he fell back to the floor. My body was no longer in my control as I ran over, straddling him, gripping his neck between my hands, squeezing with every last bit of strength I had left.

Spit spewed across his forehead. I bent down, saliva spewing from my screams.

"You did this! You made me this way! You son of a bitch! This is your fucking fault!"

My words bounced across the walls, echoing like a cave, surprising even me. But my hands clenched down even tighter, watching his face color as he fought for his last breath. The life in his eyes drained, a sight I had become too uncomfortably familiar with. My hands fell from his neck onto the floor below. I panted in exhaustion.

Sitting back, I stared at his lifeless body. A minimal disturbance of pain rose and fell in between my heavy breaths, but it was tolerable. My life, everything that has ever happened to me, this was *him*. It started with and needs to end with him. I never wanted this, I never intended for this to happen. Staring at him opened the uncomfortable truths about myself that I had yet to face. I have been fighting the grayed fine line of who I wanted to be and who I *am*.

My hands lifted to my face, the very forces of destruction that have impacted so many in my life. The blood that stained these hands could never be washed, never concealed. I have been revealed as everything I never wanted to be.

My gut jerked and tears cascaded down my cheeks, still observing my shaking hands. The tears scorched my face with a sweltering sorrow. Leaning back, I gently laid my head against the floor, looking up at the flickering light still pestering. Any thought of the creature, Jim, all washed away in the sorrow I felt for a life I wanted to return.

Every ounce of energy I had left was consumed, evaporated under the weight of my emotions. I closed my eyes and lifted my hands atop my chest, folding them on top of each other. I was to wait for the return of whatever shall be. The journey has become much more than I could bear. My eyes drifted further back into my head as sleep waited for me.

A rustling noise in the distance startled me awake. My toes curled, my body stood still, ready to flinch at any sign of distress. The rustling grew closer shifting to footsteps. Several of them. The footsteps neared closer, but I locked my eyes shut and pursed my lips together, not wanting to see my fate.

A sweet voice called out to me, starting as a delicate whisper.

"Lyle, Lyle, where are you, darling? Lyle? Ah there you are, honey! I have been searching for you! Where did you run off to? You had me worried sick! You mustn't do that to me, worry lines are very unsightly."

It was *she. Clara*? Her laugh lifted me in a way I hadn't felt since I was a child. I could hear a smile cracking in her voice. I wanted to open my eyes, but my mind needed to be sure. My body sank into the floor, my toes uncurled, wanting to believe it was her.

She continued, "Let's get you up from there, honey. Dirtying your clothes like that only gives me more work. Here, I know! Let's dance!"

I felt a soft hand reach for mine, assisting me up from the floor and slowly to my feet. My eyes remaining closed, I couldn't let go of this moment.

"Did you forget how to dance already? Fix those arms silly and lift your neck. Be confident, bold, remember? One. Two. Now step."

Clara's words caressed my wounded heart. The smile beaming on my face held back the tears threatening to fall. I had missed her. Her warmth, her humor, her confidence.

"Eyes up, darling, feel the music. Let it flow through you, with you! There you go! One. Two. There you go!"

Breathing in, I could smell the sweet scent of her perfume wafting toward my nose. I took in more, reminded of how elegant the smell was. The touch of her skin, her scent, her voice, all had been forgotten, pushed back and replaced by darker thoughts, images, visuals I would have prayed to forget. This is what I wanted to remember. This is what I needed. I pictured her in that yellow dress, a silhouette formed at the top of it, barely giving sight to her neckline. Her wide-brimmed hat with a ribbon tied around and the high-curved heels, she stunned at any event. This is how I wanted to remember her. This is how I was to picture her. Her beauty locked in time, never warping, never altering, transfixed in this moment. The faint sounds of "Come Josephine" broke through the atmosphere as Clara hummed along.

We defied time; whether it stood or passed expeditiously, it didn't matter. I was firmly planted in the moment, letting it lift me in every way. I felt her hand reach to my face, lifting it. I lifted my own hand, folding it over hers as it rested against my cheek. As a little boy, she would rest her hand on my cheek, letting me know everything would always turn for the better, even when it didn't. Her comforting touch was all I needed to continue.

"Lyle, my dear, you have to open your eyes. You cannot see with your eyes closed. Open them, please, honey?"

The soothing voice of Clara slowly evaporated into a voice I no longer recognized.

"Open your eyes!"

The raspy voice screamed in my face. Alarmingly, the formerly smooth hand felt rough and frigid. Her sweet scent was now masked by a musty, dark scent, irritating my nose. My eyes shot open, aghast at what was before me.

The frame of an decrepit old woman with greasy straw-like hair and a vindictive masculine jawline stood before me. Her vacant feline white eyes were impossible to stare into as chills penetrated my body. Wrinkles and spots littered her body as I pulled her hand from my face and leaped backward, allowing as much space between us as possible. She let out a bellowing laugh that exposed her grated teeth under the thin, bloodless lips. The sporadic flickering of the lights added to her grotesque appearance. She motioned forward, creeping toward on her spindly legs like an aged spider toward its prey. My eyes searched for an exit, seeing a glimmer of what could be a door past her shoulder.

The body of Jim flashed into view, which I had forgotten under the spell of her malevolence. But there was something off about it. It *wasn't* Jim. But the time was apt for me to leave. If I didn't move, I might never leave.

She grew closer, reaching her bony spotted hand toward me. Quickly, I darted to my left, pushing past her, finding the door, and quickly exiting the room. I made no efforts to examine the body. My mindset was clear: escape. I slammed the door behind me. Her menacing laugh echoed through the walls, flooding my ears.

CHAPTER TWENTY-SEVEN

"LYLE? MR. LYLE! THERE YOU are! We have been searching for you! What are you doing *here*? How did you find this area? It's normally closed off. It's forbidden! We must leave this instant!"

Dr. Holmes?

I turned from the door to see the hallway had been transformed back, upright, as the asylum always was. Dr. Homes, Joan, and Marc hurried forward, panic visibly written all over Joan's face, her forehead covered in worry lines.

"Was this all a part of your plan, Lyle? To get us down here, rile us up, and to have us searching these endless hall like fools for you? Well I found no humor in it whatsoever, Mr. Lyle!"

Joan's voice quivered.

I was at a loss for words. I couldn't be sure if they were real. If any of this was real. I wanted to reach out to touch Joan, but touch no longer was indicative of reality. My mind was distrustful but my heart was relieved to be out of that hell.

"Do you have anything to say for yourself, Lyle?" Marc furiously questioned. "You had Joan worried sick. And Dr. Holmes and I searching endlessly through these damn mazes to find you! I cut up my left leg, and we lost Richard." He pointed to his torn left pant leg indicative of a cut.

"Since you have been wandering these halls, have you seen him? Or are you two in on this together?" Marc's voice lifted to a sincere sternness that I was taken aback from. Maybe he was a man after all.

"Yes, Mr. Lyle, have you run into Richard? We seemed to have lost him along the way and have had no such luck in finding him," Dr. Holmes nervously stated, peering around abruptly, refusing to make eye contact with me. Peering at him, I noticed his body was facing toward the wall in a readied stance, looking to escape if need be. His fidgeting hands became a distraction as I tried to search for words to say.

"No," was all I could muster in a raspy tone. My throat scratching from the varied screams. I quickly lifted my hands to my throat, horrified.

The screams. My throat. All of it. Christ, was this real? Is this real? Are they real?

My mind searched for answers, wondering how I could tell if they were here with me and not going to evolve into some horrid creature.

"No? *No?* Is this all you have to say for yourself? After everything we have—"

Joan's words were cut short by Dr. Holmes's hands as he lifted them in the air.

"Joan, it is fine. If Mr. Lyle hasn't seen him, then I will continue the search for him after we safely return you to the exit. Mr. Lyle, I will be returning you to your room and we will discuss this matter later. Now, follow me. We must walk, *quickly* now."

Dr. Holmes didn't even turn to see if we were following, he hastily moved forward, leaving this hallway behind. His eagerness to leave the area was perplexing, but after what I had encountered, I made no efforts at a fight.

"I said quickly now!" he yelled back, nearly running out of the hallway.

Motioning my hand forward, we all quickly raced to catch up with Dr. Holmes. A sudden scattering noise in the distance behind us fell faint. Immediately, the three of us stopped only turning our heads toward each other, I nodded back at them and we locked our eyes forward, refusing to look back in collective agreement. Whatever I had experienced, they had encountered something as well. And I needed to know.

Impulsively, I ran up to Dr. Holmes, "Stop! I need to—"

"There is no time for discussions right now, Mr. Lyle, we can speak later. We just need to leave this *area*, quickly now. All of us, come on! No stragglers."

Frustrated, I fiercely grabbed at his right wrist, turning him toward me. Now, face-to-face.

"What in the hell is *this place*, huh? What has you running so scared?"

"We need to move. I'd be happy to speak to you at a later time, but this is not the moment. Now, if you will, please release my wrist so I can continue."

Dr. Holmes pulled at his wrist, taking a step forward, but I was dissatisfied. I needed to know more. Yanking him back, I pressed him against the wall.

"I don't think you are hearing me, Doc. There's fear bleeding through your eyes. Joan is scared out of her wits, Marc is bleeding, and Richard is missing. Isn't that a little strange for even you?"

"I don't like what you are implying."

My face met his, my right hand moving at lightning speed from his wrist to his jacket collar, lifting him up by it.

"I have just, nearly, walked out of the seven stages of hell back there, with my Goddamn life still attached. So I'd really like to know what in the fuck is happening. I need some Goddamn answers and you are going to give them. Now!"

My mouth roared in his face, shocking even myself.

"Or what? You'll kill me? Like all those other men? How many were there, *James*? Your father, did you kill him, too? That's all you know. That *is* all you *are*."

His words stung deeper than I could have imagined.

Slowly, I loosened my grip on his collar. The room fell silent. In the corner of my eyeline, I could see Marc and Joan bow their heads, looking to the ground. I turned my eyes from Dr. Holmes, dropping my hands to my side.

"Good. Now that we have all this cleared up. We need to—"

Before Dr. Holmes could finish his words, a hushed knock emanated from one of the rooms behind us. My heart jumped out of my chest, pinning me to the floor. My eyes focused on Dr. Holmes, his on mine. He was fighting a rising panic, his hands jittering. Attempting to calm them, he pressed them firmly against his side.

In percussive succession, louder, more thunderous knocks spoke to us, gaining our full attention. Turning in unison, we all stared at the door carefully opening, teasing us through its slow movements. The door I nearly escaped from. The door with *her*. Noticing Joan's wobbling legs, I placed my left hand at her base and my right on her forearm, ready to catch her in the event she collapsed. Marc's body ran cold, the life draining from his face, his eyes sealed dead ahead. I shot a look at Dr. Holmes, waiting, praying for an explanation, anything. But terror stole his words. He lifted his hand to his mouth, too frightened to utter a sound.

My arms grew exhausted but were tense, waiting for what may appear. The anticipation, it was thick in the air, ready to slice at any moment. Calamitous thoughts plagued my mind. The visuals were vivid and surreal, forcing me to remind myself that they were only in my mind. I wanted to turn back, to exit the hallway, but my feet, my body, it was responding to my commands. We were *stuck*. Browsing the other's faces, their bodies, I could tell, they too desperately wanted, needed to leave. But we couldn't. It felt as if a force was anchoring us down, chaining me to this spot. The time egged on. I could almost hear the ticking of a clock marking our time, from seconds to minutes. The time drew on. The door remained boastfully open, sinking me further into despair with every passing second.

The expectancy, the dread lifted its wave, soaring in unimaginable heights before finally falling. A slow and steady creak made its way to my ears, heightening my senses. The familiar sound sent a shock wave of angst. The sound quickened its pace as out of the room, a wheelchair appeared, steadying itself before slowing to the middle of the hallway. My right hand still holding Joan's arm, I squeezed tightly causing her to groan in agony. But I didn't let go. I was transfixed on the sight.

Tommy?

Tears rained down Joan's face, wetting my hand as she tried to pry against my clutching fingers.

"Lyle, please, please let go. Please, Lyle, please!"

Her pleas broke my trance to see her tear stained cheeks and wide-eyes, my fingers were wrapped tightly around her wrist, visibly marking her.

Swiftly, I removed my hand from her arm, releasing her from my distressed grip. She rubbed at her arm, pulling it into her chest. I quickly peeped at the chair, feeling my legs desire to move, I rotated my body back to Dr. Holmes.

"What is this? What is happening? Is that . . . is that Tommy's chair?"

He remained silent, mute, his stare never lifting from the chair.

"Damn it, man!"

I pushed him against the wall, slapping his face to look at me. Gaining his attention, his eyes widened as ours met.

"What the fuck is this? Is that Tommy's chair?"

I lifted my hand again, burying another slap across his face.

Red appearing on his right cheek, his eyes browsed from me to the chair, back and forth, unsure of where to look. I lifted my hand for another blow but his mouth motioned for words, stopping me from striking.

"It . . . it can't be," he stumbled in his words.

"What do you mean?"

Grabbing his collar in my hands I pushed my forehead into his.

"Look at me, damn it! Look at me."

I smacked my head into his, forcing him to look directly into my eyes.

"It can't be his. He's . . . he's dead!"

His words nearly shot my legs from underneath me. The blow I hadn't anticipated. Pushing him back into the wall, I flung my hands to my chest, unsure if I could breathe. A baseball developing at the rear of my throat. My stomach violently churned.

My knees gave way smacking firmly against the concrete. My mouth dropping, letting out a lingering wail.

My nose puffed, blocking my efforts to breathe. My hands searched for my hair, pulling painfully at it. I clutched my eyes shut, hoping this was a dream.

Dear God. No! No. Tommy, Tommy can't be dead! No!

My heart sank into the bowels of my stomach. Feeling a sudden touch of warmth on my shoulder, my body flinched in reaction, sliding off the gesture. It was Joan. I knew it was. Her warmth radiated a different type of energy. But I wasn't ready for it now. My mind was caught between thoughts of killing myself or killing Holmes. I was wrestling with something so gruesome, my stomach gurgled in response, threatening to vomit if I continued pursuing these thoughts.

"I am so sorry, Lyle. I know words may not mean anything to you at this moment, but I understand your pain."

Joan's right hand gently lifted my lowered head. I looked up into her watering eyes. Her hands cupped my face as her thumbs rubbed against my cheeks, wiping away the fallen tears. My hands slowly lifted to meet her wrists. I held them softly between my hands, allowing her sweet gesture.

"My God."

Dr. Holmes's words dropped like a weight in the air. The hallway fell dark, immersing us in an abyss of terror. I jumped to my feet, wiping my tear-stained cheeks with my left palm. Joan held tightly my right arm to her chest. Her body eased into a rhythmic tremble. Only the white of her eyes were visible.

The sound of a bell ringing three times set me for a pause. I wanted to be sure I had heard this and it wasn't my worried mind playing tricks at the helm of the darkness. I listened intently, turning my head to avoid any obstruction. Three rings repeated, in a slower pace. One. Two. Three. A subtle sound. Could have easily missed it if we were distracted. But I wasn't convinced I had heard this. I needed more.

Marc clarified for me.

"Did you all hear that? What is it? A bell?" he whispered.

"I don't quite know. But we need to leave. We shouldn't be here. Please, everyone, let's quickly lea—"

A hushed silence fell over Dr. Holmes. Through the opened door, a shadow of flickering lights projected onto the hallway wall. At first, it was just a consistent light, flickering on, then off. But deep within my bones, I could feel something more was approaching.

"We need to back up slowly. Do you all hear me. Slowly start moving backward. We can't be too hasty. We don't know what may happen," I repeated in a hushed tone. Joan frantically clutching at my arm, I reached out my left to feel for Marc.

"Yes, indeed. Let's back up," Dr. Holmes agreed with a whimper.

I could hear Joan's shallow fast paced breaths. She had roped both of her hands around my right arm, her head leaning into my shoulder. The flickering continued with three more bell sounds starting up. Quicker in pace. Consecutive sounds, ominous, and succinct. I reached again for Marc, still searching for him in the dark.

"Marc? Marc, I need to know you are here. Are you moving back? Where are you?"

The flickering bright light ceased, stopping us all in our tracks. Joan poured her head deeper into my upper arm. I flailed my left arm, searching for Marc in the darkness, only catching cold air.

"Marc, this isn't funny, please, Marc, where are you?" Joan's voice cracking mid-sentence.

"*Here.*"

A thunderous growl blared through the halls washing over my face. A blinding light broke through the room, revealing Marc standing at the entrance, facing the opened room. My eyes widened, ready to explode out of my head, confused, petrified.

"Marc? Marc, what are you doing? Get away from there! Get back!"

I motioned to take a step forward. Marc's head contorted from his body, cocking at me, only a shadow of his blackened eyes were present. His malicious grin haunted me. I felt a tugging at my shoulder as both Dr. Holmes and Joan pulled me back.

"Marc, honey, what are you doing? Marc, please, get back here. Please."

The pain in Joan's words were lost in his face. That smile, those eyes, that cocked head. I needed to look away. I wanted to look away. But I didn't. I couldn't.

I motioned to take another step forward but Dr. Holmes quickly grabbed my shoulder and pulled me backward.

"He's too far gone. Don't look. Don't look. We need to move and move now. Move, move, move, please!" Dr. Holmes nearly screamed in panic.

He had to keep pulling me backward as my legs forgot how to move. I was attuned to Marc. In the bright lights, in a flashing instant, Marc's face returned to the opening as he was pulled in. The door slamming shut behind him. Dr. Holmes pulled harder, turning me away from the door as we hurried forward. I motioned my head to look back but Dr. Holmes caught my face, pushing it forward.

"Don't look back! *Never* stare. Just keep going. This is our chance!"

Joan's heels were slowing her down but she kept moving, pushing her legs and lungs to fight against staying in this hell. I held tightly to her hand, nearly sprinting from the area. The hall felt endless. I worried we may have been trapped, but we finally came to a white door. Dr. Holmes hurried himself through, nearly shutting us out but I pushed my arm out, stopping the door from closing on us. With Joan and I in the room, I slammed the door, ensuring it was firmly shut. Turning away, I dropped Joan's hand and leapt into Dr. Holmes's face, pushing him backward. He fell to the floor, his hands raised.

"I should kill you! You were trying to leave us in there! And Tommy. . . I . . ."

"Lyle, we can't worry about this now. I don't feel safe in here either. We are only a heartbeat from that room. Let's do this somewhere, anywhere else, please?"

Without Joan's pleas snapping me from my thoughts, Dr. Holmes was about to be killed.

I glared at him but Joan grabbed at my hand, "Please, I don't want to be here anymore."

My eyes removed from Holmes to Joan; I nodded to her.

"Where do we go next? She needs to get out of here."

Dr. Holmes, still holding his left hand up for protection, slowly rose to his feet.

"Why, yes, yes, I quite agree. Through this door, we must exit. It'll take us back to your wing, then I can escort Joan out."

Dr. Holmes took a step toward another door but I rushed him against the wall.

"No, no. I need to see that she is safe. Do you understand? I will walk with you to ensure she leaves safely. Do you understand?"

His eyes switched between mine and Joan's as he searched for words to say.

"It's not possible, I assure you." Nearly aghast at the thought.

I lifted my forearm across his neck, pressing into his throat.

"Make it possible." I pushed in a little deeper.

"Fine! Fine! Just unhand me!"

I dropped my arm and backed away. He straightened his coat and motioned toward the door. Opening it, I turned back to Joan.

"After you."

CHAPTER TWENTY-EIGHTEEN

SHUTTING THE DOOR BEHIND ME, I was relieved to be putting more space between myself and that hellacious hallway. We entered a new hallway, one that rang familiar. This was the hallway of Beast. I vividly recalled locking eyes with that monolith of a man. His stare, the smile, it was unforgettable. Just as most events here are. *Evil, it lives here.* Whether in a person or the unknown, it is here. And it will stay with me until the day I will die.

Joan was situated in-between Dr. Holmes and I, still clutching at my hand. With each hand squeeze, I could tell her nervousness was getting the best of her. Another hour here and she may go mad herself.

Approaching the cell where Beast was caged, I mentally prepared myself for what I would see. Coming closer, I could see the outline of a figure in the room, but it wasn't clear yet. I sped up my pace, wanting to face this man, unafraid, and with conviction. I wanted to speak with him, to know his story. I needed to understand.

"My God!"

Dr. Holmes approached the cell first, stopping dead in his tracks, his hand covering his mouth.

"Please shield your eyes. Lyle take her—"

Before he could finish his sentence, I yanked Joan away from the sight, covering her eyes as we walked forward.

Joan let out a whine, "Is he—oh my God, he's dead isn't he? He's dead."

I could feel the warm tears gathering underneath my fingers.

"Shh, shh. Let's not think of this. Just keep moving, focus on my voice, alright? Just keep your focus on me, I'll guide you. We are almost at the end. One step at a time. Nearly there. Perfect. Now, Joan"— removing my hands from her eyes, I stepped in front of her, tilting her face up—"I'll be right back. Promise me you will not move? Promise me?"

She nodded quickly, tears streaming down her face. She caught them with her left hand, wiping with the back of her hand, then dropping her head.

"Are you going to be okay?" I asked.

She nodded, still staring at the floor. My finger caressed her chin as I stepped away, returning to Dr. Holmes who had entered into the cell.

"He was strangled. Look, you can see the marks around his neck. Someone was atop of him, bearing all their weight down. My God, how?"

My eyes widened, shooting open at the sight.

Dick?

He laid there, wide-eyed, and mouth still open. Finger imprints dug deeply into his neck. I moved in closer to see a belt buckle unfastened from his pants clutched in his right hand.

Dear God.

"But how could he be in here? Why? This doesn't make any sense. He was with us until the lights fell."

Dr. Holmes stared up at me, jaw dropped, still in disbelief. He stood up from the body, taking a step back before turning to me. His eyebrows shot up.

"Unless, would you happen to know anything about this? You disappeared on us, God knows where you were. There was no love lost between you. This wasn't you, *was it?*"

His words rang into the back of my head as Dick's dead body seeped deeper into my thoughts.

The belt. He was strangled. No, this can't be? It's just not possible? It was Jim. It was Jim I killed!

Moving past Dr. Holmes, I dropped to my right knee, examining Dick's body closer. His neck was bruised, echoing tightly held fingers and a thumb imprint into his Adam's apple. His neck had been squeezed so tight it looked like it had been crushed. I leaned in closer, staring into his eyes. Lifting my hand, I laid it on his ice-cold chest. He was freezing; he must have been dead for some time.

A flash of light burst in front me, blinding me. I lifted up my hands, blinking my eyes shut. Shaking my head, I squinted my eyes open, noticing something moving below me. The frame slowly came into view as my eyes adjusted to the dark atmosphere.

Dear God!

It was Dick. I was straddled above him, hands clenched around his neck, the veins in my arms ferociously popping up from my skin. His mouth fell open and a deep gasping noise was made. His eyes ran bloodshot, the vessels ready to pop. He was smacking at my arms, flailing around, even attempting to whip me with the belt, but my grip only tightened. No matter how many times I repeated to myself to let go, to stop, the squeeze only tightened, digging deeper and deeper into his neck.

The burn marks from my fingers interlaced around his skin. The sound of a pop emanating from his neck allowed my hands to fall. At that moment, my arms fell to my side, now in my own control while his body seeped into the ground, wide-eyed and slack-jawed.

Christ. What have I done?

It was no secret I had wanted Dick dead. But I wanted to change. To prove to myself that this wasn't of me anymore. I wanted to be better. To prove to myself I wasn't what they thought I was, who *I* was beginning to *think* I was.

Tommy and I spent endless hours complaining about Dick, but I felt I had put those vitriol feelings behind me.

"Lyle, if you kill him, you'll just go ahead and prove them right." Tommy said, earnest in his tone. "Everything they say about you, all of it, it's now true. Don't give in to that, don't give them the damn pleasure. Y'er better than this. What you did in the past, that was a by-product of your experiences. Many of those men, they had it coming."

"And Dick, he doesn't? That asshole finds any reason to inflict injury on me. Beating me with that club and extending those fucking treatments. Last week, I was sure he broke a rib or two. He doesn't deserve the air he breathes."

"You always say y'er not the monster everyone makes you out to be. By killing him, you prove them right."

"What if I am Tommy?"

"What are ya saying?"

"What if I, what if I am that monster?" The words echoed gravely.

My shoulders slumped and my body fell to my right side lazily, slumping off of Dick. My palms rose to my eyeline.

What if I am that monster?

Fixated on my hands, the sight of them flashed under the quivering light hanging above me. My stomach fell. Through the crevices of my hand, I realized where I was. Or where I had returned. The room's full view lifted from the shadows.

No, no, no, no. Not here again. Fuck. Fuck!

I motioned to stand up but a firm hand pressed itself into my left shoulder, startling me. My chest lifted and my body stiffened. My breath quelled. The clutch of the hand dug deeper into my shoulder, nails pressing inward.

My mind scalded my legs for not moving, running out of there, but my legs were paralyzed in terror. Working through my thoughts, my mind begged for a steady resolution. Taking a deep inhale, I counted down from five, readying my body to leap from the floor to the door.

Five. Four. Three. Two.

I held my breath as I could hear a dragging sound surrounding me.

One.

I opened my eyes and she was there, her left foot dragging across the concrete before she situated herself. Bending downward her feline eyes seared into mine. Now at eye level, her white eyes were tombs of desolation, of desperation. Her crooked smirk nearly wiped the thoughts of escape from my mind. The beating of my heart against my ribcage exploded in my chest.

Her face drew in closer, her decrepit skin moving into view. Her mouth opened, exposing her grated teeth. From the corner of my eyes, I could see her right arm lifting, her boney long fingers ready to strike. Her left hand fell to my head, pinning me deeper into the ground, panic flaring in my soul. Sealing my eyes shut, I focused on my breath, wondering if these were my final ones.

"Forgive me," I mouthed.

The overtaking of a roaring shrill muddled my thoughts, and I embraced for her strike.

"Are you ready for the leucotome, Dr. Holmes?"

The words drifted in and out. Sounding distantly in an echo chamber, and unfamiliar.

"Not quite, almost do—Ah! There! Yes, now, please. Thank you. Note the time will you, Richard?"

"Writing it down now, sir. 2:30 p.m., Wednesday, August 23rd, 1943."

"Mr. Lyle, I have inserted this tool into your head. If you can hear me, do not try to move as it will be in vain."

The voice shot me back from my slumber but my eyes remained forcibly sealed.

"I've injected you with a few substances. Quite mundane, I can assure you. A wonderful combination of cocaine, heroin, and a Nitrous Oxide anesthetic shall keep you quite comfortable, I suspect. But please let me know if the pain becomes unbearable, if you can, of course."

He laughed.

"Now, this may feel uncomfortable, but you shall not move, I need your full cooperation for this to be successful. Do you understand?"

He paused in expectancy but my mind could not process how to move my mouth. My mind was overwhelmed. Everything was happening too quickly for my head that fell miles behind.

"This procedure, here, will help ease those terrible hallucinations and sounds you have been hearing. This may even relieve some of the other ailments you have not spoken of but I have detected. Don't tense your body, my dear. This will be over soon and you will feel grand! We need to rewire many pathways in your brain that allow you to, so easily, harm others without reproach. Do you understand, Mr. Lyle?"

Hours must have passed as my legs melted into the gurney at a standstill.

"As you know…" he grunted. An uncomfortable push sent shockwaves throughout my body. "We have tried so many other approaches with you. Ah, yes. Richard, hand me that. Thank you. For which all have been in vain. But this one, I have hope. I made a promise to make you better and I will strive for this, if it's the *last* thing either one of us do."

Somehow his words did not provide the relief he was aiming for. On the contrary, my mind raced, trying to conjure through the failed experiments he had tried, all of which were beyond painful and hellacious. I could not reason with myself if dying was the better alternative in living here with Satan, himself, in this living embodiment of hell.

"All done! You were an excellent patient today. Wait here, and soon you can return to your room for a peaceful slumber."

He patted my shoulder.

His steps retreated and the sound of a door creaking open, then the slamming reminded me that I was still alive. Attempting to lift my hands to my chest, I felt a constraint. My hands were tightly wrapped under straps, rubbing eagerly against my skin. A burning surge raced against my wrists as they throbbed in tenderness. The wearing effects of the drugs started to wear off and a deep reverberating pain climbed upward into my skull.

CHAPTER TWENTY-NINE

I CAN'T REMEMBER WHEN I had eaten last or even had a sip of water. My mouth dried up in thirst as I swished the tiny bits of spit I had left around in my mouth. My dried lips burned while I pressed them together. Gnawing pangs of hunger rumbled in my abdomen, confirming I was, indeed, alive. For now. But what was real? The defeating thoughts galvanizing between reality and dreams spurred a deep unrest. The beating drum in my temples blared painfully under the guise of this treatment.

I had noticed my heart rate quickly fall, nearly coming to a quick halt. A heavy liquid seeped from the crevice of my mouth, cooling my overheating body. The room shook like an earthquake ascending upon us. My eyelids rolled between open and shut, the force too burdensome to remain fully open as the room was spinning with each open eye. An unpleasant rumble in the pits of my stomach forced my hands against the straps, the pain nearly unbearable. The jolting of my body against the gurney struck thunderous bolts of agony in my head.

"Damn it, Lyle! Nancy, quick, get a doctor in here! Now! Quick! Christ, why? Why did you have to do this? I thought you were off of this shit!"

My head bobbled back and forth but a cool liquid dripped onto my forehead.

"I called the doctor, he is on his way, Mr. Wallace."

"Nancy, fetch more cold wash clothes, he's drying these up like a sponge! And grab a pillow, I'm going to turn him on his side."

My body drifted onto my left side, my eyes too heavy to lift.

Shuffling footsteps and a bursting through the door was followed by a wringing out of a wet towel.

"Put it under his head there! Yes, there! Easy now! This damn boy is going to send me to an early grave!"

"I'll hold him still, Mr. Wallace. I also flushed the remaining items down so he cannot access them anymore."

"Heavens, there was more? Thank you, Nance. Between all the booze and drugs, he is becoming my full-time job! When he comes out of this, make sure to remind me to have Helster on him more. Every move, every breath he takes needs to be watched, guided carefully. We can't have these events happening anymore. One more like this and it'll kill him!"

"Of course, sir. I think I hear the door downstairs, I'll fetch the doctor up here!"

"Hang on, Lyle. He's almost here. Damn it, boy. All I do for you and you do this? I should disown you."

His words quivered but steps piled in and his voice drew back, returning to its normal tone.

"He's done it again, Doc. Help him, please."

"Right away, Mr. Wallace."

A calming sensation lifted through my sore body, providing the relief I was urgently craving. Time passed while my body relaxed. An unintelligible symphony started in the background trying to cover the voices as they spoke. But the words still towered over the music.

"Mr. Wallace, I understand you love this boy here, but he needs some real help. Abuse, addiction such as this is not to be taken lightly. Many have succumbed to this type of lifestyle. He has too much access to certain people, money, perhaps. Maybe limiting what he can do, who he can see, we can slowly ween him off? But if he continues, I'm afraid, he will die. I have no doubts. We, I can help him. I have a state of the art institute where we can house him. Temporarily, until his addiction is kicked. Please think it over, Mr. Wallace?"

"Thank you, *Dr. Price*. I just don't think that is the best option for my boy at this time. But if it continues to worsen, I know where to call."

"Of course, sir."

"I appreciate you making some time out of your schedule to be here these past few weeks. It has been just as hard on him as it has on me. Your institute shall expect a sizeable contribution, I assure you."

The words drifted from ear to ear, my mind shouting from all corners, but my mouth remained mute.

"Thank you for your generosity, Mr. Wallace."

"Nance, here, will see you out. Good day, Dr. Price."

The door opened with the sounds of feet exiting the room before it was closed once again. But a lone pair took a step before pausing.

"Lyle. Christ."

The steps returned, moving closer before stopping behind me, my back facing toward the sounds. The creak of the floorboards beneath me under his weight lifted as he dropped to his knees.

I felt the damp cloth wash over my face, allowing one eye to slowly rise open. Charles's worried face blurred into my sightlines while the other eye fought to open. My hair was gently brushed out of my face; Charles's fingers cool to the touch.

"I have failed you as a father. I have. I'm sorry. I promise to be better. I do. You are all I have. But I need a promise from you. You need to be better to. This shit will kill you. It will. If something is wrong, come to me. Not *that*. To me. You understand?"

His voice ceased due to the shivering in his voice. His water stained eyes drifted to the window, fighting against the tears aiming to flow down his cheeks. Charles was not an emotional man. He prided himself on staying collected, even under the guide of death or sorrow. But this time, this time he let himself feel.

Any words I had disappeared under his emotions. My eyes filled with water and my nose became stuffy. He returned his eyes to mine because I reached for his hand, nodding toward him.

I needed to be better. The life, the choices, they were eating at me. Tearing me in half. The secrets of the bodies piled in my head. The unspeakable actions, even if deserving, was a cross I was struggling to carry. My heart sunk deep into my chest as I knew this warning, this plea, as touching and heartwarming as it was, was never fully accepted. I would go on to disappoint Charles. Disappoint myself. Crawling further and deeper into the abyss. An abyss that I could not find myself out of.

Staring at Charles, my tears at a standstill, I wanted to savor this moment. More than anything, I missed him. My heart ached wishing this was where I was, where I could be again. But I knew the moment would disappear soon bringing me back to whatever reality *IT* wanted to torture me with next.

A small smile drifted onto his lips, pushing my hair out of my face. He didn't say it, but I felt it. His love. A fathers love. Someone cared if I had lived or died. The feeling overwhelmed me but I valiantly fought against the rising tide of emotion, not wanting to disappoint Charles and his brave bravado.

"Let's get you from this floor and into some better clothes, shall we? No son of mine shall look like this."

We both chuckled briefly while he reached out his hand and gently helped me to my feet. The nausea still swam eagerly in my bowels. Nancy walked in and helped me to undress, cleaning me with a towel from the urine and vomit seepage. Charles walked to the closet, searching for some garments to place me in. Nancy was careful with me, as she had been many times before. Careful in turning me and washing me delicately to my sensitive skin.

Her smooth skin masked her age. She was well into her fifties, but only the white in her updo exposed this. She had the kindest eyes a woman could have, a soulful brown. She wore her wrinkles with pride, her confidence never looming. Her lavender perfume started to mask the former harsh flavors I had smelled of.

"I'm sorry if I dirty your dress, Nancy."

She loved her old floral dresses, always refusing Charles's gifts of new, designer brands. She was a simple old woman who basked herself in kindness.

"Oh, my dear. No need to worry yourself about this. I have plenty more. And I can wash it. You know how well I can wash soiled clothes."

Her kindness reflected in her smile.

"We just need you better, all better now. It worries me to see you like this. I've watched you since you were a young boy but don't think I can't put you in your place as a young man now."

Charles had hired Nancy to help his late wife care for their child. But after their deaths, he kept her on to help with me. She was the grandma I never had. I wish I had told her that. I wish I had told her how much she had meant to me. All the nights I would come in, bloody, a mess, never a question on her lips. Only the offering of help. She would dispose of my clothes and send for new ones. She must've known, she *had* to. But she never let it show in her interactions with me. Up until our last moments together, she was always her warm, kindly hearted self.

Charles returned to the room with a casual suit and some polished loafers.

"How about this? Not too much, I hope?"

"No, not at all." I said.

"It's perfect, not too tight around his waist and still have him looking as handsome as ever." She placed her right hand against my cheek. "A handsome man such as yourself shouldn't be mixing himself with things of this nature."

I drifted into her hand, lifting mine to cover hers. I nodded.

"Good. Now that it's settled. Dinner, tonight? We must celebrate."

"What are we celebrating, Mr. Wallace?"

Nancy turned her head toward Charles, helping me into my shirt.

"Life, of course." He beamed a reassuring smile to me.

CHAPTER THIRTY

THE VIOLENT TREMBLING OF MY body must've made such a noise to send Dr. Holmes back into the room, racing in with a syringe.

"Grab ahold of him, Richard. I need to get this in steady. Get ahold of him, now! Steady. Steady. Ah, yes! That was a close one, Mr. Lyle. Let me check your pulse. Let's turn him over, he will be vomiting soon, I suspect. Get him some water, he looks absolutely parched."

My head was lifted, tilted slightly to allow the water to gently stream into my mouth. The overwhelming pleasure my dry mouth felt when the first drops drifted onto my tongue was immense. My cracked lips were overjoyed. I lifted my head, begging for more.

"Not too much, Richard. Easy. Go slow. Ah, that's enough for now. We shall give it a few more minutes and return with more. Mr. Lyle, I will be right back. I have untied you from the straps, but do not try to escape *again*. There are dire consequences, and in your weakened state, I don't feel you are up to facing them. We can leave him."

My body was riddled in agony, trying to turn into different positions, without falling off the gurney, seeking any fleeting moment of comfort possible.

But the torturous feelings never dissipated. Loads of vomit raced from my stomach up through my throat then down into a bucket placed below me. My eyes blurred with tears. The vomit continued, spewing for what felt like hours. My head felt like it was bursting in flames. Its competition through pain was met by my stomachs burn. I wasn't sure if I wanted Dr. Holmes to return or if his absence was an unintended blessing. I lifted my hand, searching for one of those damp clothes to wipe myself with to no avail. I needed to lift my head to search for something. My body was heating up again at a rapid pace. A fever was pouncing on me. The weakened condition of my body made it immensely difficult to lift my head, making it feel like bricks of weight weighing me down. Struggling, I lifted my chin, able to finally find the bucket of water and clothes. I grabbed hold of the buckets handle and slowly brought it to my gurney.

The water was dirty and foul, but the aching thirst and heated temperatures were nefarious. I wrung the towels out, dropped them on my head and neck areas before lifting the bucket to my face and drinking from it. As horrid as the water tasted, it felt as if a fire had been put out. My body relaxed back into the gurney, allowing me to wipe my sweat-filled brow with the damp clothes. My erratic heart calmed, allowing me to lay my head back against the gurney.

Dr. Holmes returned, praising his efforts at healing me.

"See, my dear! All better! Now, give him some more water Richard, and we can slowly return him to his room."

I wanted to spit this water back up into his face for leaving me in this condition without water. He probably knew I would drink from the bucket. Dick unfastened my feet from the gurney, allowing me to finally move them. They were tender and pink from the overly-tightened straps. Lifting them up off the bed onto the floor felt foreign but relieving. The blood rushed back into them, providing them with the strength they needed to take the next step.

"Slowly, now, Mr. Lyle. Move too fast and you just may collapse. One step. Then the next. That's it. Nice and easy."

I used the surrounding items near me to hang on as I refused Dick's assistance. My head was slowly spinning. The pounding in my head was returning, making my body sensitive to each step. I had to stop to take account for the blaring knocking overtaking my entire body. It was torturous, mind-numbing. My mind couldn't comprehend further; I stopped remembering how to walk. My chin lifted to Dr. Holmes and our eyes fixated on each other, him studying me. His expressions said what I couldn't. Something was wrong. Something was terribly wrong, and I had no way of uttering this out loud. My legs halted in place, feeling like sandbags as I attempted to lift my foot for the next step. But they didn't budge. Blinking rapidly, in trepidation, I tried to adjust my eyes as my vision was disappearing. My body jittered uncontrollably, painfully. My vision narrowed to just Dr. Holmes. The oceans of ice in his eyes sank me deeper into the darkness.

Dr. Holmes's lips slowly moved, but his voice was lost in the realm of delirium. "...are...alright...Richard...help...get...he's..."

My mind scrambled his image, blending him into the fog eclipsing my sight. My hearing collapsed, the sound of my thudding heart pulsated in my ears. A thump here, then a long wait, before numerous thuds followed. There was no consistent rhythm, scaring me more than I had ever been. I felt my head leaning forward, my body swaying, my hands miraculously still gripping onto whatever I had available for balance. But the grip loosened, each finger slipping. My weight pressing me forward, I smacked against the floor, sending a feverous blow to my head. I was conscious for a brief moment but my head whipped forward, sending me into the black.

"Lyle, Lyle! What have you done?"

"I...I haven't done a thing. He just collapsed. Right there. We were standing here and we were talking when he bent over and fell forward, hitting his head onto the floor!"

"We need to get him up, to help him! We can't leave him here with this dead body!"

"Mrs. Tracey, we can and we need to. I need to get you out of here and return this asylum back to an orderly fashion. My assistant is lying here, strangled to death, next to the man who I believe to have committed the atrocity. And—Oh, dear God. Mr. Harold. This is his hallway. The hallway of the undesirables."

"Undesirables? Doctor, how can a person be considered undesirable?"

"Mrs. Tracey, the human mind is complex. Some suffer from minor abnormalities, but others, like him and Blackman, they are of a different breed. Nearly inhuman. Unapologetic, void of empathy or sorrow. Their only programmable traits are destruction, chaos, and infliction. Wanting not only to kill, but to make suffer. This is their game, the both of them. The two are locked away in this specific hallway because *even I* cannot help them. God, himself, could not return these beings into men. Mr. Harold was sentenced here for unspeakable crimes. Blackman, well, his story is unknown. In fact, we don't even know his real name. He hasn't spoken a word since he was committed here. They have killed, Mrs. Tracey. Here. In this very asylum. Not once, not accidentally. Viciously. Heinously. Mercilessly."

"Excuse me, Dr. Holmes, but you aren't making any sense. I thought this asylum was run on a tight leash? Now you tell me you have two complete psycho's who have killed while detained here?"

"Some things are better left in the dark."

"And, Doctor, there is no one in here. This hallway was completely empty when Lyle walked me down it. You must be mistaking this with another area."

"What do you mean the hallway was completely empty?"

"I mean just this, the cells were open, not a soul inside any of them."

"Oh, dear God. If the two are not—we need to go, Mrs. Tracey."

"I'm sorry?"

"*Joan*, we need to go *now*. I need to phone the police. It is not safe here. Not now. Lyle is one thing, but these beings, they are sent from the depths of hell. I have been working Mr. Harold and Blackman for decades and they both only seem to worsen with time."

"No! No! We cannot just leave him here! No! We need to get him up and take him with us. Look, he obviously needs a doctor to attend to him!"

"I am a doctor!"

"A *real* doctor! Not some man who speaks with loons all day! People don't just collapse for no reason! Especially with that monster running around. No. I refuse. He needs to come with."

"Joan, Joan, my dear, you don't seem to understand the gravity of the situation we are in. As I mentioned, these are not just some ordinary lunatics off of the street. Or some killer like Mr. Lyle, here. No, damn it, they are something I have never seen before. Untouchable, damn near unkillable. And either of them will rip us both to shreds, then consume us after if we do not get ourselves bloody out of here! Now take my hand, Joan, we are leaving! Now!"

"Unhand me, you fool! Unhand—look! Look! Lyle, he's, he's getting up! He's coming around. Look! He's shaking his head. Let go of me, now! Oh, Lyle, let me help you, honey. Don't try to lift your head too fast. You have a nasty gash there. It's bleeding pretty good. But I know a great doctor who can help you. A *real* one. One who can get you out of the madhouse and into some real help."

Her words were faint but I was able to follow them. Her cool hands caressing against my cheek while my head lay in her lap bided my time to come fully awake. To come to.

"Leave him, Joan! We need to leave. We don't have much—oh, no! Someone's coming. I told you to leave! I *warned* you!"

Dr. Holmes voice fleeted. The sound of racing footsteps echoed down the hall. He had left us.

"Lyle, honey, I need you to wake up. Right now. Please, we need to get out of here. Immediately. I can hear *something* coming. Please, wake up, wake up, Lyle! Wake up!"

Her gentle taps turned into slaps, forcing my eyes open. An ominous whistling emanated down the hallway, creeping closer. Joan's worried hands tried to lift me, but my body was not yet strong. My head fell back into her lap.

"Lyle, I need you to help me. I cannot do this by myself. I am not leaving you here, not with those *things* on their way. Please, find it in you to lift yourself up. I'm begging you, for both of our sakes!"

She whimpered in a hushed voice. The whistling edged closer, putting both of us on edge.

I raised my right knee, hoping to gain some leverage as she lifted under my arms, but I slid back down. We tried again and again, continuously falling. Then the whistling stopped. And I knew. *Someone* was there. Someone who was not Dr. Holmes.

The energy, the presence, was different. Behind us. A leering stare set my back ablaze. Long winded breaths heated up the room. Joan clutched at shoulders, panic seizing in her mind, clouding her judgment. I grabbed onto her arms, turning her from this thing to behind me. Whatever was to come, I wanted to make sure I was first. My arms slowly maneuvered my body to face toward him, my legs curling in to turn.

The figure was held in the darkness, a shadowy presence. Joan's hand ran to her lips, sealing them to prevent her screams. His shadow loomed, sending us both into the depths of darkness. I've seen him before. This wasn't the man they called Beast. No, this was someone else. A man who had no name. His familiar tortured body and ghostly pale skin reminded me of our first encounter. And I think he remembered too.

That low growl of his sent chills throughout my body, lifting the hairs on my arms. Joan poured her head into my back, her whimpers vibrating against my spine. His black eyes dug into me, still without a blink, and again, swallowing me whole. He carefully dropped to his knees. Eyes still peering at me, the whites accented by the blackness of his iris. His coarse hair whiffed back and forth as he crookedly crawled toward us, his whistling starting back up. I pulled my legs up to my body and my left arm out to shield Joan. She tightly wrapped her arms around my waist, audible sobbing sending warm tears down my back.

"Please, please. Don't hurt her. It's me you want. I can take it. I am the guilty one. But don't hurt her. She is innocent of this."

I lifted my right hand forward, pleading with this *man*. His rigid face lifted upward, revealing an ambiguous smile. He crawled even closer, meeting me eye to eye. Joan's nails sliced into the sides of my abdomen, my trembling hand retreating to my chest. The rotten odor of his breath against my face was enough to churn my stomach. He even smelled dead. His knife-like fingernails traced against my cheeks as his gaze left my eyes and fell to my features. I braced tightly for the dawn of a painful and gruesome death. My eyes only seeing him through squints of vision. He deepened his nail into my cheek. I could feel a small warm liquid drip down my cheek.

I was sure Joan was ready to collapse in exhaustion, but she held up, tightly clutching against my waist, my only reminder that he hadn't killed me yet. He lifted his nails from my cheek, turning his eyes back to mine before letting out a bellowing laugh. Like a spider running across the room, he crawled backward, exiting the room, that horrifying laughter following with him.

We both let out audible gasps. Our sighs filled the room with a warmth that was surely missing. How we escaped the painful disembodiment by a horrifying psycho is a question I will bring to God, or the Devil, whomever I meet first.

Joan's sobs rang in my left ear, her grip loosening from my waist, now clutching at my hand. She needed to still hold on to me, to feel my body. She was terrified. Without a shadow of doubt in my mind, this was the closest she has ever come to real fear. Real evil. Politics can bring out a certain type of evil in a man. But this type, this was *the evil* you hear in ghost stories. The one you pray to never encounter. Monsters exist. They are here. And she has now seen them, too.

My heart's thunderous beats quietly slowed to a sensible rhythm. But my guard was still up. Beast was still out there. I had never seen him before, only heard the legends of him from Tommy and a brief run-in on his massacre. As much as I feared whatever that *man* claimed to be, I feared Beast much more. There is something beyond fear, beyond terror, about an individual who relishes the thought of ripping apart people, still alive, then consuming their flesh. With him, Joan and I would stand no chance. I know he would not let us off with a warning. He would strike, having Joan watch as I was ripped to shreds, my shrieks blaring as my blood painted the walls.

But I needed to be careful with what I shared with Joan. Turning back to look at her, she was a frazzled mess. Her makeup running off of her face and her glass-stained eyes still welling with tears. She was breathing open-mouthed now, her nose stuffy from her crying. She looked a mess. Defeat and anguish washed away her beauty. She was walking that fine line of barely holding on and tripping into madness.

"Joan, are you alright?"

I turned my body toward hers, rubbing my hands against her arms, but she did not look up. She nodded, her head tilted downward, cowering against me.

"Thank you for not leaving me. I overheard you. With Holmes. That was incredibly kind. Selfless." I grabbed her hands, pulling them up to my face, planting a kiss on them. Her eyes still locked downward. "I don't think anyone would have done that for me. Not one. But you did. I may not make it out of here. But I promise you will, understand?"

She slowly nodded her head but I needed her to truly grasp the feelings behind it. Her act of defiance and her willingness, albeit incredibly moronic, was touching to me. So many that I have loved and who claimed to love me, all of them turned their backs. It is rare to find someone who would give themselves for you. I had pegged her wrong. She was something special. She *is* something special.

Wrapping my right hand under her chin, I tilted her face up toward me. Our eyes met and I was overcome. I leaned in, pressing my lips deeply into hers. She pressed into me further, the raw emotion overcoming us both. My mind was tangled between the thoughts of her soft lips and how her taste lifted a piece inside of me.

We didn't come up for air. Joan let out a deep inviting moan. She wrapped her arms around my neck, pulling me in closer. I pulled my lips from hers to breathe her in. Her gorgeous neckline had been teasing me. She smelled of jasmine flower. It was hypnotic and overpowering. I wanted more of her. Laying my lips softly against her neck, I felt her fingers run through my hair, pulling it backward, desperately aching for me to return to her lips.

I obliged, the taste sweeter than before. The forbidden fruit ripe to be eaten. She dropped her hands to mine, positioning my hands for her liking. My fingers slipped beneath her hem but she didn't flinch. Wet and eager. Begging for me. Her moans beckoned me on. She wanted more. Anxiously, she pushed her undergarment away, catching around her ankles. My lips pressed back into a sly smile while my hands quickly fell to my trousers. It had been such a time since I had touched a woman, felt a woman, been inside a woman. I was stiffened, roaring to go, ready to unleash my inner desires inside of her.

But before I could reveal myself, the room darkened in an ominous warning. An eerie silence draped over us, pulling me out of the moment. I wanted her, I needed her. But this was not the place. Not now.

Damn.

"Joan, Joan, darling. I want you, I do." I lifted my hands up, a type of surrender. "But I want this to be special, somewhere romantic. Not in a dingy cell with a couple of psycho's running around. Let's get out of here first? Then I promise, I'll make it up to you."

I pulled her garments back up then placed a gentle kiss on her forehead. She looked disappointed. Her eyes dropping to the floor, a frown populating, but I think she understood. The act would leave us vulnerable, distracted. And in a place such as this, that can be deadly. I made my way up from the floor, leaning my hand out to help her up. She dusted off her dress and grabbed onto my hand. We turned toward the open cell door, unsure what awaited us next.

My left shoulder felt a tight squeeze from Joan's fingers turning my head to look back at her, giving the go-ahead that we were to continue forward. Our first few steps were leery, carefully watching over our shoulders. Quiet in each step, we barely pressed our feet against the floor to avoid making too much noise. I was a heavy stepper and Joan's heels were a dead giveaway. Luckily, she had removed them prior to walking out, both of us walking on our toes, step-by-step.

"Do you see anything," she whispered.

"No, and I think that's for the better. Keep quiet, we don't know what could be lurking around the corner."

"Yes, but do you even know your way around?" she asked insistently in a hushed tone.

She was right to ask; I wasn't fully aware of where I was taking us. The halls are endless here, mazes into the unknown. Some hallways lead to nowhere, others to identical corridors. The design must have been crafted by a madman. I remember Dr. Holmes mentioning Dr. Price had been a key figure in the development of this place in the late 1800s: "Dr. Price was instrumental in the building of it all. The layout, the architecture. The design was inspired by the madness of our patients. It doesn't always make sense, you may get lost, trapped even, but in the end, you may find your way out. Through some difficulty, naturally." He would laugh. "A man may enter sane but leave totally mad after walking through these halls."

How those words stung now. I had always wondered what became of Dr. Price. Did he, himself, lose his mind here? Is he now a victim to his own design, lost in the madness? His body was never recovered. Tommy mentioned that his disappearance was without explanation, without recourse.

"Hey Tommy, what do you think happened to dear old Dr. Price?"

"Oh, without a doubt in my mind, he is dead. He knew too much of this place and wanted to shut it down. It was in the newspapers for a short time, all the crazy experiments and controversial tests people were subjected to. Dr. Price made quite the unusual statement that it wasn't under his doing, those happenings, ya know?"

"So what do you think, Holmes killed him?"

"Naturally. Who else had so much to lose but so much to gain in his death."

"I wouldn't put it past that crazy bastard. It's funny."

"What's funny, ya madman?" Tommy playfully yelled through the wall.

"The Doc condemns me for killing a few bastards, calling me downright evil. Yet him—"

"Shit, Lyle. You know men. We are quick to cast the stone but can't seem to look through the glass at ourselves. And, if it makes ya feel any better. I don't believe you to be evil. Not in the slightest."

"Ah, Tommy, thank you. Are you getting soft on me in here?"

He belly-laughed but his remarks were what I needed. All the alone time I have been cruelly subjected to had me wondering if I was not only crazy but evil too.

"Of course not, you rat bastard! When we bust out of this prison, the next round is on you, whaddya say?"

"Of course, Tommy. Of course." My words echoed my smile.

My memory of Tommy quickly fell back to this hell hole and how Dr. Holmes quickly took over, as he had been Dr. Price's understudy, keeping the disappearance a hushed secret and mingling relationships with those in power. This hell should have been condemned decades ago, but Holmes's airtight alliances kept this place a well-known secret with many blind eyes.

"Lyle, my feet are freezing and the halls all look the same, are you sure you know where we are going?" She tugged at my arm, turning me to face her, pulling me from my thoughts.

Annoyed, I peered at her.

"Do I? No. Not in the slightest. But as long as we remain alive, that is my first priority. I am looking for something familiar, something that will give me a clue as to where we are. And I haven't found it just yet. But I assure you, doll, when I do, you will be the first to know. Now, please," I leaned into her, noticing how unfair I had been in my comments. I placed my right hand on her cheek, caressing it with my thumb and said, "Please remain quiet. I don't want anything to happen to you. I know we will find something soon. But if we have to, we can rush into any one of these doors or cells."

I tilted her head up toward my face, our eyes meeting, "Please stay close, okay?"

She nodded with a smirk. I bent down, placing my forehead onto hers.

"Let's keep moving, hang on to my hand."

We entered a new hallway but it seemed familiar, eerily so. The temperature dropped a slight amount, clueing me into where we may be. But I needed to be sure. As we passed each room, some empty, some with people inhabiting them. Harmless individuals. Crazies but not full-blown psychos. They all paid no mind to me. A few laying on their beds staring up at the ceiling, another sitting in the back corner, only his feet were visible, and one man who pressed his face against the glass pane to get a look at Joan. He stuck his tongue out licking across the window. His obscene gestures after had Joan blushing in embarrassment as I laughed.

The next room, however—its contents halted me in my tracks. A wheelchair. Could it be? *Tommy?* I rushed up to the window, tapping my index finger against it, but the body did not move from the bed. I wanted to get his attention, needing to know if Tommy was still alive, or indeed dead, as I recalled Dr. Holmes sourly informing me. But I couldn't remember if that was in one of my many altered states or if this was in this particular one. My mind can no longer distinguish its sights and sounds from the different worlds. They have all blended into one for me. But the question still remained, eating away at me, Was this Tommy?

Taking an unmitigated risk, I turned, kicking open the solid door to the horror of Joan.

"Lyle," she slapped my arms, "what in the hell are you doing? Are you trying to get us killed?"

I subtly pushed her back, mule-kicking the door once again at a furious intensity. The act was already dangerous, but if I was already participating, I needed to fully commit. Nervously, I turned back to the window, peering inward, waiting for a sign. The figure inside rustled in its bed, carefully sitting up, his face shielded in darkness.

"Lyle, can you let me in to whatever the hell you are planning. It involves me too, you know? Your actions can have me slaughtered and eaten as a main course. Please, what is going on?"

I didn't face her, only muttering, "This could be Tommy. Tommy?" I repeated.

"Who in the hell is Tommy? And why are you risking my—our lives for him?"

Her condescending tone didn't sit well for me. As much as I liked Joan, Tommy was my best friend, my only friend in here. Talking to him through these walls, the jokes he would tell, the laughs he gave me, despite everything, are memories I will treasure. She is just some broad I just met. If it came down to it, Tommy would be who I save.

"Tommy! Tommy, can you hear me?" I yelled into the window. "It's me, it's me, Lyle! Tommy, is that you?"

"*Lyle.*"

An unfamiliar man's voice called behind me. I turned around to see who could have possibly said this. The words were felt on the back of my neck, as if a man had calmly repeated my name next to my ear. But there was no one else there. Joan and I were alone in the hallway. I hoped.

"Did you hear that, Joan?"

My eyes scanned the hallway, the lights a fluorescent dimmed color, difficult to see past a few dozen feet.

"Hear what?" She seemed genuinely confused, turning her head to follow my eyes.

"My name. Someone said my name. Right here. It sounded like it came from right here." I pointed to the floor, showing her how close that voice sounded.

"Lyle, you're scaring me. What do you mean you heard your name?"

"Joan, I heard my name, clear as day behind me. I know it."

"I didn't hear a thing other than your unceremoniously obnoxious noises from kicking the door that I am sure will get me killed."

I know I heard it. Plain as day. My name.

Shaking my head, I faced toward the window but was immediately startled, falling a few steps back. There was a face in the window, eyes staring back at me. Joan let out a scream before quickly covering her mouth, the echo of it tracing down the hall.

"Tommy? Christ! Is that you?"

I ran back up to the door, pulling at the handle. But it would not open. Leaning back, I used all the body weight I could to pry it open, but to no avail. My hands reached up to my head, clutching my hair in frustration. Pacing back and forth, I tried to think of a plan.

"Is that even human? And why would you let him out? Is he dangerous, Lyle?"

"No, he's not dangerous. He just looks a little pale, a little worn out. That psycho Holmes has been experimenting on him for God knows how long and its finally done this to him."

I pointed to the window, but Tommy's face was no longer looking through. It was empty.

"You saw him right? Right there in the window." I pointed forward. "Tell me you also saw a man looking out?"

"Yes, Lyle. This time I did see him. He scared me. He didn't look friendly. His eyes. His eyes. Must we open this door?"

She wasn't in the wrong. Tommy's appearance even startled me. His face was gaunt and ghost like. His eyes were oceans of ice. He looked nearly dead. His boyish looks had drastically faded, aging him twenty to thirty years. I wasn't so sure if what was held behind this door was even Tommy anymore.

I studied Joan's worried face; her brows lifted in a constant state of uneasiness. But I wasn't sure what to do. Tommy is my friend. My only friend. He wouldn't leave me. He is loyal. The only person in my life to be that way. I couldn't betray him by leaving him here. That would make me just like everyone else. My hands clenched behind my head while I pondered my next move.

The steady exhales of Joan and my breath were interrupted by the unlatching and creaking open of the door. Tommy's door slowly opened. My mouth fell slack-jawed and Joan ran behind me, gripping anxiously onto my arm. We waited for the door to fully reveal what was behind. I stood in a readied stance, hands up, but eyes bracing for an unwelcomed visitor.

The room was dark revealing only a figure sitting in a wheelchair at the entrance of the doorway, the white of his eyes only visible.

"T-t . . . tommy, is that you?" I surprisingly stuttered. Nerves were running through my veins, quaking through my voice.

I waited for a response. Letting the silence cut through the air. It was penetrating, adding to the uncomfortable aura. The words finally came in a hushed raspy tone that I didn't immediately recognize.

"Ly—" he sighed, having trouble with his breathing. "Lyle? Is . . . that . . . you?"

I moved closer, Joan still at my heel, following like a shadow, never relenting from her grip.

"Yes, Tommy, it's me. Are you okay? You look , , , different. Unwell. What happened?"

"I . . . feel . . . different." He spoke in flustered pauses. His voice was cracking. But it was him. A *different* version of him.

We creeped in closer, finally reaching him at the door. I pushed the heavy door to the side and pulled the chair into the hallway. It was Tommy. But he didn't look as he did in the window. His color had returned, his face round. I didn't know to be terrified at what he was or relieved at what was before me.

"Lyle," Joan whispered gently into my ear, "that's *not* the same man we saw in the window. Not even a little bit. What is happening?"

It was not the same man in the window, and I was thankful for it. Damn my eyes. I was just happy to see Tommy again and adding to Joan's frazzled nerves were of no use. I needed both of them to remain calm while my mind attempted to sort out what was happening before me.

I bent down, leveling myself to Tommy's height.

"It's so nice to finally see you, Tommy. It really is. When did they move you into this hallway?"

Eerily, he slowly lifted his head to meet my gaze. He had a puzzled look on his face.

"Move?"

"Yeah, Tommy. When did they move you here? Do you happen to know why? All of our endless night talks getting on their nerves?"

I tried to laugh it off, but the look on Tommy's face was concerning.

He cleared his throat, taking a deep inhale.

"I haven't moved. I've always been in this room."

"Ah, come on, Tommy, such a kidder you are. Now, really, why did they move you to this hall? The freaks are loaded in here."

"I'm"—he paused as to carefully word his sentence—"not sure what you are suggesting. I have *always been here*. You, too, have always been here. That's your room next to me."

He pointed at an opened door to the right just a few steps down.

I stood up, glaring at the door. This area was so unfamiliar. The men caged in the rooms. I had remembered a fairly empty hallway. Lockehart, Tommy, and myself. When did this happen? Tommy seems confused. He doesn't look well anyway. He has to be confused. He must be.

But my eyes never wavered. It almost felt as if the door was also staring back at me. Pulling me inward. Wanting me to take a look. Without notice, my feet moved toward the door. Before I knew it, I was standing opposite of the entrance, taking deep inhales, nervous as to what I would see. I cocked my head back. Joan was standing at a lengthy distance opposite of Tommy, arms crossed, pressing against her chest. A concerned look was all she gave, too frazzled to speak. Tommy had returned his head back against his chest, too heavy to keep ahold of.

My feet side-stepped the door, moving toward the opening, my left hand running across the metal material, it was cool to the touch. Surprisingly, my heart stood at a steady pace. But I wasn't in control of my actions. It was a pulling that I cannot explain, a magnet of some kind.

Most of the room was held in darkness with only a quarter of its entrance visible under the light. My right foot stepped inward, then my left. I was submerged in the room. It felt unfamiliar, unlike what I remembered. But it was mine. The sheet, the layout, my book, all of it, just as I had left it. My mind could not understand why this room felt unfamiliar, distant, strange. Had I been gone so long I no longer recognized my own room? Or is this even my room?

I moved in closer, sitting on the bed, the familiar creak paving its way into the long-held silence. My head drifted downward, searching the contents below, confirming that this is, truly, my room.

Why? Why can't I remember? Why?

My head poured into my hands, rubbing my palms deeply into my eyes in frustration.

What is happening to me?

My skin burned from the relentless rubbing between my eyes, begging for me to stop. I released my hands, eyes still shut, allowing the burn to slowly dissipate. Just as my skin was starting to calm and my eyes feeling the weight of the pressure resolving, I felt a finger hoist my chin upward. I figured it was Joan coming in to remind me of her sweet presence. My eyes still held shut, my left hand reached for hers.

"Joan, your hands are awfully cold. Here, let me warm them up."

I leaned into to breathe warmer air on her hands but the sound of her screaming in the distance shot my eyes open. There before me, the entity had returned.

The creature and his blue eyes. The white lines surrounding his eyes reminded me of veins of ice in a deep ocean. I was trapped in them, it was all I could see. We were eye to eye, locked in battle to see who would waver, who would blink first. As if they were pried open, it never blinked. Stone faced. But my eyes fought heavily as my eyelids started to fall. The weight becoming overbearing. Tears developed, ready to fall when my eyes closed completely. I strained, too afraid to close my eyes, unsure of what *IT* would do.

Joan's screams beckoned me again, a call for distress. My body, however, was invisibly chained to the bed. I could not move my arms nor my legs. I motioned to open my mouth, wanting clarification from Joan, needing to know what was happening. But *IT* lifted its frosted finger to my mouth to silence me. *It* hushed me in a voice that sent shockwaves through my body. That voice was not the entity's.

"Lyle. Oh, how I've missed you."

Audibly, I gasped, breaking the stare. The voice's familiarity sunk deep into my stomach.

Charles?

The creature smiled, nodding in affirmation, as if he had understood what I was thinking. His wide-mouth smile was pasted on a leathery type of skin. His overly-large gap teeth lurked beneath his menacing features. My mind shut down, unable or too horrified to process the rest of what I was seeing. My eyes wanted nothing more than to look somewhere else, anywhere else.

Joan's wails pierced one more time through my ears, striking deeply into my head. The strength in my legs returned and I lunged forward, pushing *IT* back, sprinting out the door. *It's* eyes were felt deeply in my back but I dared not turn around, too afraid to see the rest.

Scanning my surroundings, I noticed a trail of blood leading to Tommy's room.

Christ, he's killed her, hasn't he?

I cannot recall running into the room or how I felt. My mind fell blank. The blood splatter, the pieces of flesh scattered about the room. A finger dropped before me, rolling toward me. The events surrounding me moved at a slower pace, winding down with every passing second. It didn't feel real. I didn't feel a part of the monstrosity. Almost as if I was watching from above, a type of scary story playing out before me. But I was a part of it. I was in it. And it was happening in front of me.

There was the *man* with no name. Like a wild monkey, he leaned over what was left of Tommy, having been ripped to shreds. His chair looked as if it was dipped in blood. The crunching of bones and ripping of skin. I wished I was deaf at this moment. The eating of a human body, of my best friend. I fell to my knees, a pain punching at my gut vociferously. The chewing sounds finally getting to me. The burn of bile running up my throat and spewing in front of me. My eyes welled, a pain so recognizable. My heart felt as if it had been ripped out of my chest. This too, familiar. Everyone I have loved. Gone. All of them. My head lifted to see the *man* unaffected by me, tearing deeper into Tommy's stomach, tugging at his insides, voraciously consuming him from within.

The tears dried in my eyes, my fingers balling tightly against my palms, digging deep inward. Tommy's voice circled around me, surrounding while I slowly stood to my feet. A sincere conversation delving into my complexity and tragedy as a human being. "That isn't you anymore, Lyle. That *was you*. You can change it. You can change who you are, Lyle. Don't give in."

This is who I was and this is who I am. Who I have always been.

My feet flew into a frenzy, charging at him. As fast as I was running, everything felt slowed. I was able to catch every glimpse of Tommy's broken body laid out throughout the room. Rage, hatred, ferocity increased with each step. My purpose was known. My intentions were clear. The rush of euphoria whipped deep into the air. My lungs inhaled, holding tightly onto the feeling, closing my eyes, salivating in the moment. The world around me had fallen dark. A darkness takes over, blinding me of my own actions. It sweeps over like a dust storm, temporarily leaving my world sightless.

Time stood still. My vision had been restored. I had no more thoughts, only visuals, images to take in. Relish. The *man* was laying beneath my feet, his ogled eyes looking upward, wide-mouthed but his body bent facing the floor, lying prostrate. His neck was twisted in a tightly held position. I bent down, reaching the back of my hand against his cheek. Cold. He had been dead for some time. The warmth drained from his. The life vanished. My eyes met in unison with my lifted hands. They were calm, steady, pulsating from pressure, reddened from friction, but unwavering. My body trembled coming down from an ecstasy.

Execution was more than a drug, it was an addiction. I tried to explain this to Tommy. I cannot control who I am. I did not choose this. Everything that has happened was done unto me. Transforming and guiding my soul. Evil lives in all of us. But there is so much more than this. Acting upon those evils, that is what separates each being. I have fought against my natural desires for so long. Masking my true self under the realm of what is expected of me. I cannot help who I am. I make no apologies anymore. The shield has fallen. The mask has been lifted. One still remains . . .

"Dear God, Lyle! What have you done? What—you—monster!"

From behind me, Joan's words carried to my ears. But I could not help the smile from engraving on my face. Cocking my head to the left, I turned to face her. Dr. Holmes was quietly coming up from her side, his mouth fallen in awe.

"What in the bloody hell? Mr—Goddamn, James Lyle! You murdered this man! Did you kill your friend, Tommy, too?"

Holmes pushed Joan to the side, walking an aggressive pace toward me. He lifted his index finger and pressed it against my chest, his face entering into my space. My eyes fell to his finger. Glaring. The gall.

"Did you kill him too? Huh? Richard wasn't enough for you, you blood crazed animal. You needed more? Answer me dammit!"

His right hand pressed firmly into my chest, catching me by surprise. My head whipped from the side, leering back into his eyes. My breathe took a deepened tone and my knuckles whitened.

"It wouldn't surprise me one bit. Killing your 'friend.' You killed your father, Charles, didn't you? Didn't you, you will answer me when I'm talking to yo—"

More than enough of his angry spit had splattered across my face. Before he could finish his sentence, his neck was firmly resting between my hands. I could feel the vein in his neck pulsing against my fingers. His eyes looked ready to pop out of his head. Hoisting him up from the ground, the echoing retreat of Joan's footsteps thrilled me. I could kill him without the guilt of traumatizing her.

I wanted to snap his neck right there. His feet dangling in the air, eyes ready to burst, veins bulging. But he deserved more. So much more for the endless torture he put me through. All I had endured. I deserved to inflict much more.

"I promise you, you will die. But it will not be like this."

The disdain breached through my words. I was the living embodiment of vile.

His face turning into a purplish-red hue, my arms catapulted him into the concrete wall. His shoulder split directly against the hard bearing, giving way. The crackling sound of the separated shoulder was music to my ears. A beautiful symphony had begun. And I was in the front row. Ready and excited for the show to commence.

"What, Doc? A little broken bones too much for ya? Aren't you supposed to be a real doctor? How about the sight of blood, how are you with your own?"

He wailed in agony. A sickening look gave him away. The sight of blood from others was fine in his mind, but his own, I had a feeling he never had the pleasure.

"Well, let's just find out now, shall we?"

I crept toward his broken body. His reaction had me embarrassed for him. He begged, pleaded with his remaining good arm. He wanted a reprieve.

"Doc, I hate to break it to ya. You are praying to the wrong man. I am not God."

I punted his good arm. His shrill nearly cracked my eardrum.

"If I'm going to hell, I'm dragging you down there with me."

As I was bending down, a reflective piece caught my attention.

"Ah, you brought a knife to the party. How considerate of you! Now we can really get started!"

My smile oozing into my words, laughing maniacally I lifted the knife from the floor and lunged toward him. My physical exertion thrusted the knife, mistakenly into his left thigh. I was aiming for his abdomen.

"Boy, I sure do hate mistakes, don't you? My apologies. I was aiming a little higher. Forgive me."

His glossy eyes were fading, he was losing consciousness. The pain may have been too much but I was not done.

"No can do, Doc. We have so much more to discuss. Wake up!"

My hands slapped against his cheeks, momentarily waking him. His eyes rolled forward, but he was losing touch with reality. I needed to bring him back. I stood up and stomped my right foot into the knife, sending it deeper into his thigh. He awakened. Roaring in pain, tears cascading down his cheeks, vomit erupting from his mouth. Half of him was drenched in sweat while the other half was dipped in blood.

"There you are! Glad to see you are still with me. I'd hate to see you miss all the fun. Now, usually I don't talk when I am about to kill someone. I prefer not to. Makes the act too personal. Remains in my mind too long affecting my sleep. I like to sleep. Peacefully, too. But with you, Doc. I have so much to get off of my chest. All this time, biting my tongue, biding my time here. Counting down the days for when I could finally kill you. And now it is here."

My arms lifted upward, "Thank you."

All he could mutter was a fumbling version of "monster."

"No, Doc. You are the monster. You inflict endless amounts of torture on the vulnerable, the unwilling. I inflict on the deserving. Who's the monster now?"

His eyes fell from mine but he gurgled his throat, letting loose a ball of spit into my face. My smile quickly drowned into fury. I lifted his white coat and ripped from his undershirt a piece of garment to clean the spit from my face. His visible chest was beating at a rapid pace. If I didn't kill him soon, the wound surely would.

"Wrong answer, Doc."

I thrusted my fist against his abdomen, knowingly breaking a rib. His mouth fell open to cough but only a drip of blood poured out.

"You have whipped me, submerged me in ice, held me in bondage for days at a time, outstretched my body, and performed various painful and ineffective surgeries without the pleasure of an anesthetic. But this is just my pain. The bodies may not line the halls like mine do in my own criminal record, but we both know who you are, Doc. You're no better than me just because you have a fancy title and a white coat. Evil runs through these dying veins. Even more so than mine. Dr. Price and all the men you have killed in this hellhole. Be sure to give them my regards when you meet them in hell."

I lifted his head and hoisted it against the wall. His skull cracked loudly against the concrete. His head fell forward revealing a red painted imprint.

"How about one more for good measure? What say you?"

I gripped onto his head, ready for the final blow.

CHAPTER THIRTY-ONE

CLICKING SOUNDS ONLY A FEW steps behind me followed by an unfamiliar voice stopped me dead in my tracks.

"Don't ya move another fucking muscle! Don't ya do it! I'll blow y'er head clean off, ya hear me?"

The words hoisted me backward, into a memory I had prayed I would forget. With my eyes clenched closed, I already knew where I was. The wind chill of the freezing temperatures placed me at my end. Slowly, I opened my eyes, revealing the outside of an aging church blanketed by the falling snow.

"Freeze, James Lyle! You are under arrest! Do not move or you will be shot!"

I had posted in a prayer position for hours, awaiting their eventual arrival. Time was the only obstacle. I was numb, frozen, but not just from the winter weather. Tears had tattooed icicles on my solid cheeks, so heavy I thought they would fall. I was on my knees outside of the church, kneeling on the layers of snow building on the walkway, fixated on its majesty. The large Roman Catholic church and its cross bared down on me, judging me before it. I did not enter. I had intended to when I made my way, but the sight of its grandeur was not a welcoming host for someone like me.

I was—am tainted. My prayers are whispers into the abyss. No one is listening anymore. There is no savior for the damned.

The bell tower rang letting me know it had been hours since Charles last took his final breath. I turned to my cold, wicked hands. Sprinkles of white dusted over my open, reddened palms. I lifted my head up to the sky and allowed the snow to beat down on me. I was ready to die that day. Frozen outside of a church, God's storm punishing me for my crimes. Even the snow could not blanket my sins.

"Lift your hands atop of your head, boy. But don't you even think about moving a thing, ya got it?"

My fraught silence fell in the air, only moving to lift my hands, dropping them on top of my head. My eyes never wavered from the church. A little hill of snow developed at the base of my nose, but my body already ran numb. There will be heat in my next life.

"Petersen, head down there and cuff him. Do it quick now. Ya hear? I'll watch for some funny business. But don't trust him. Not even a little. He's dangerous. Understand? Now go!"

The crunching sound of footsteps broke the solemn silence in the air. My frazzled voice broke out of its reserve.

"Oh God, why have you forsaken me? Why? From the start it has been a tragedy. One that I have not asked or wished for. Why, God? Huh? Tell me! Give me a reason. Give me something for this hell I have been put through! Answer me!"

My hands dropped into prayer hands, my eyes welling with tears, my voice cracking under the scream.

"Put your Goddamn hands back on top of your head, boy! Do you hear me? Do it now or I'll fucking shoot!" the officer roared in the distance.

"Go ahead. Shoot. I'm *already* dead. Doesn't matter anymore," I retorted solemnly, slowly rising to my feet, hands outstretched.

"Stop. Now. Please, or I'll have to shoot!" The officer walking toward me hesitantly breathed, barely audible.

"Come on! Do it! Kill me! Come now, shoot me, damn you!"

I dropped my hands to my sides, facing the two officers and their drawn guns.

"Kill me!" I screamed, nearly bursting my vocal cords.

The officers did not move. They remained in their gun-drawn stance, the younger cop wavering in his tracks. A rookie, possibly? His lack of confidence exuded through his lack of eye contact. But my stare remained, locked onto him. A predator watching his weak-minded prey. He wasn't going to kill me. It was not even a thought in his mind. His outstretched arms were shaking. His aim would be inaccurate in his nervousness. He was petrified.

"You're no killer," I pointed to him, smirking.

"Me?"

"Shut up, Petersen. He's trying to bait you. Stand your ground and keep your mouth shut! I should've brought Bronson. Damn him!"

"Yes, you. Petersen, is it? Son, you're no killer. I know them. *You* are *not* one of them." My words shot deep into his heart. He nearly dropped the gun as the words sat in the air.

"Shut up, you loon!" The other cop cocked his gun. "Take another step and I'll shoot!"

My eyes turned from Petersen to the other cop. A large overweight fat man. Older, hair as white as the snow falling carefully hidden under his hat. His knees were falling weak. His time had come and gone. He wasn't looking to make a name for himself today. Killing me wasn't on his mind either. I deepened my stare as I took a step forward. Daring him to shoot, but he didn't. A couple more steps and I would have been within arm's reach. I tossed the idea of killing the two men around in my head. Half of me felt it was the right idea, a necessary one. But the other half was ready to finally give in, give up. I have become weary in fighting, pretending to be someone I am not. What had transpired today revealed to me a piece that I didn't know existed. Who I have become is everything I hated in a person.

Cocking my head, I turned back to speak to Petersen.

"Have you ever seen a dead body, boy? Hmm?"

Unbeknownst to him, his body revealed pieces of him that were meant to be in private. He shook his head. No.

"Erhm. You going to kill me now? Without even letting me stand trial? Will you not even allow me this?"

His eyes fell to the ground. I took another step closer.

The fat officer dropped his mouth open, ready to speak but I reacted before his words could enter through.

"Have you ever seen a man on his knees, begging, pleading for his life? Ever seen that? Hmm? Had a gun cocked right between his eyes and watched the 'man' in him die inside? Ever seen that? See them turn into a little whiny bitch? Shut your mouth, you fat bastard! I am not done here!" I turned, bellowing in anger at the older cop.

"Ever seen a living atheist transform into a dying Christian? No. No. I don't think you have. So who are you to come to me. Outside of this place of worship." I lifted my hands to promote the grandeur behind me. "And shoot empty threats of death upon me?"

I moved even closer, my face breathing onto the barrel of his gun.

"Well, here I am. Boy. Do it. Do it!"

I could see my cold breath blowing against his face. His eyes shuttering. I could have grabbed the gun. I could have shot him. Killed him. Quickly or mercilessly. The other officer too, probably. Neither were there to kill me. I was just a name on a paper. Who I was, who I am meant nothing to them. Just some hard-ass at the end of their shift. But I had done enough killing for the day. For a lifetime.

I noticed a wedding ring on Petersen's left hand.

"The ring." I motioned toward his finger. "Married, Petersen?"

"Yes, s-s-s . . . sir."

"Got any kids?" I questioned, needing to know.

"For God sakes man, leave the kid—"

I raised my hand to silence the other cop. Whatever look was painted on my face silenced his words.

"Do you have any kids?" I insisted, turning back to Petersen.

"Yes, a newborn. My wife and I just had a baby boy, sir."

His head sunk into his chest. This man was no killer. He was a man trying to make a wage to feed his growing family.

There is a dark side in me that is uncontrollable and ruthless. But that part, somehow, resisted the innocent, the pure. In my heart, I could not find it in me to leave a young child without a father. As cold as I had become, I knew the detrimental and devastating effects an absent father can have. The only time I saw mine was when he was at the end of the bottle or at the end of his belt.

That child does not deserve to grow up as I had. Even me, I did not deserve that childhood. It made me into who I am today. Who I hate.

"Your child shall not turn into the monster I have become. Go home to your family. They need you. This. *This*, will corrupt you. You'll meet men far worse than me. Real evil. Evil, it lives. It lives here. And it is waiting for you to find it."

His watered eyes lifted to mine. A tear dropped from the corner of his right eye, his mouth motioning to me, "Thank you." He knew I was considering killing him. He felt it, deep within his bones. And he knew I would have done it. Successfully. But for today, he can live another day for his son.

My palms clasped together, motioning upward to him. He understood. Petersen dropped his gun, holstering it back into his belt and reached for his handcuffs.

Clearing his throat, he read me my rights.

"James Lee Lyle, you are under arrest for the murder of Charles Wallace and ..."

The names read, he missed several. But hearing a handful was enough. I could be executed off of only one. But hearing Charles's name in that list tore my heart into two. He was the most prominent. The most meaningful. Not only in this city but to me. The man I believed to be my father. The man who raised me. Who sheltered me. Educated me. Clothed and fed me. He was now gone. And I had been the one who killed him.

He fastened the cuffs tightly around my wrists and walked me to the car, my legs stiffened from the freezing temperatures. My body was finally winding down, allowing the elements to consume me. Entering into that paddy wagon, I could feel the chill enslaving my extremities, a feeling I disregarded out in the fray when I was alone. My teeth chattered and my hands stung in pain. My chin fell to my chest, sinking inward as I recalled the last parts of the day.

CHAPTER THIRTY-TWO

"STEP AWAY FROM DR. HOLMES, now!"

My eyes snapped back to the asylum, Dr. Holmes's broken body below me. His laboring breaths slowing down with each passing second. My eyes lifted to the sounds. Several officers were standing just inside of the room. Four of them in total. Two at the doorway and another two a couple steps behind in the hallway.

"Lyle! Lyle! What have you done? *Why*?"

Joan's familiar voice pushed through the group of officers, her heels clacking against the concrete.

"Oh my God! Is he dead?"

Her hand reached to cover her wide mouth, in shock. Dr. Holmes was a bloody mess, but the entire room was paved in bodies and painted in a crimson red. Bodies were littered everywhere. Pieces of Tommy, the *man* with no name, and, now, Dr. Holmes, taking his last few breaths.

I stood there, quiet, unsure of what to say. What could I say? My fingers were dripping with blood. My record precedes me. I am a convicted murderer. These bodies will be tied to my name. Tommy's as well. My death was imminent. Here or the electric chair. There was no more gray area.

"Place your hands on your hand and slowly turn around. No funny business, you hear? Face the wall!"

That voice sounded familiar. His tone deepened into my thoughts as I tried to recall his face. The golden blonde hair with sparkles of white and brown eyes pieced together his memory.

Petersen?

I squinted, looking deeper at him before asking, "Petersen, is that you?"

The cops face dropped, his eyes locked into mine. At that moment, he knew. He remembered who I was. So I beckoned again:

"How's your baby boy? How old is he now?"

The confident tone diminished, replaced with that old stammer. "H-h . . . how? Oh, Christ. It's you. It's really you. *That* James Lyle!"

He dropped his right hand with his gun to his side, his left hand reaching into his hair in disbelief.

"Yes . . . here I am. Long time? So . . . how is he? Is he well?"

I examined him carefully but taking into regard the other officers' movements. They all stood there, all but Petersen, their guns pointed toward me.

"Erh . . . he, he is good. Six now . . . Very good boy. Doing well in school." His head fell again into his chest, his shame lifting through the air.

Six years old? Has it really been that long? My God. How long have I been in here? I thought it was only weeks, months probably. Six years?

My mind was racing in disbelief, trying to calculate each moment. Six years seemed out of place. I had not been here for more than a short time. I couldn't have been. I could feel a tremble building in my hands. A throbbing pulsation eerily pounded against the inner layers of my skull. It felt as if someone was kicking their way out, out of this madness?

I dare not allow them to observe any weakness. I reached my hands in front of my waist, clasping them together, shielding the noticeable trembling that was rising. The pounding in my head nearly made it impossible to think, but I needed a distraction. I retorted only what was on my tongue.

"Mhmm. Good. Nice to have a living, breathing father to tend to him all these years, no?"

He did not utter a word. His eyes gluing themselves to the floor. The officer's behind stood confused, looking around at each other, unsure of their next moves. Petersen must have been their senior.

"Not looking so good over there, my boy! What's wrong?"

The room was slowly starting to spin, my eyes unfocused. But the voice drew closer, its familiarity pulling at my soul. I could feel my body wavering. But I dug my feet into the ground below me, desperately trying to hold my stance.

"Lyle. Lyle. Look at you! A mess. Disheveled. Wavering. Mad. A Goddamn mess. Christ. I did not raise you like this, my boy."

A figure was looming in the distance but its unsteady image was difficult to piece together. But the voice... the voice I knew. I was confident in who it was.

"Charles?" I drunkenly questioned.

"Christ, boy. You cannot even recognize me? What have you become?"

"Charles? How, how is this so? You're dead? You're dead. You are not supposed to be here. How are you here?"

I stretched out my arms, hoping to catch myself in the event I fell.

"Dead? Me? I am dead? No, my boy, you are mistaken. See, me, I am very much so alive. Alive and well. Right here. I have *always been*."

"Nooo. Nooo. You died. You are dead." My words were slurring. My mouth was failing to fully cooperate.

"Dead, huh? I *just* died? *How* did I die, my boy?" His words seemed sincere in curiosity.

"You died..."

"Yes, Lyle. But *how*?" he insisted.

"You... you just stopped breathing."

"Really?"

My silence was noticeable and alarming. His voice quickened with questions, nearly accusatory before I broke down.

"It was *me*. I killed you. Yes, I did it. I didn't want to. I never wanted to. I *loved* you, Charles. You were the only father I had. But you, you *made* me do it! You betrayed me. You are just like all the others. Just like them all!"

The words danced in the air, settling on his tongue. But before he could utter a word, my legs betrayed me, collapsing below me. I laid in an outward pretzel shape. Taking deep breaths, I sat on the floor, withering away.

A figure approached, walking slowly to me. A distant snickering smile melted into his words.

"Well. Is the pain too much? Too much to bare for even you? Death, my boy, comes for us all. We cannot escape it. We cannot run from it."

The figure bent down, reaching for my legs. I desperately tried to smack away the hand, but I was now seeing double. My strength was fading and my vision was deceiving. Everything was a doubled-vision blur. The room could have been snowing and I wouldn't have been any the wiser. It looked as if everyone was caught in an epic snowstorm, blurring toward me. I swatted his hand away twice, mustering any strength, all the strength I had to push him away, but I was fading.

"He's gone mad!"

The words muffled under my falling eyes. I felt a roaring push against my chest that yanked me back against the concrete, my head snapping against it. My eyes quickly rolled back into my head. My surroundings fell quiet.

CHAPTER THIRTY-THREE

IMAGES FLASHED VIVIDLY AND OMINOUSLY before me. I could see Dr. Holmes, standing above me. He eagerly held a pick-like tool in one hand and a surgical looking hammer in the other. His mouth was moving but the words were inaudible. The pain was striking, pounding deeply and fiercely into my head. The pounding I had recognized, I felt this before. It was consistent and painfully throbbing. I tried to reach up to stop it, to stop him, but my arms were useless. They would not move. No matter how hard I tried to lift, they would not participate. They laid there, having given up, allowing this monstrosity to continue. I motioned my legs to stand, but they too refused.

My peering eyes scanned my surroundings, but the images failed to process in my mind.

What is happening? Why can't I get out of this? Wake up, Lyle! Wake up!

My body felt paralyzed with every inch that he dug deeper. My thoughts were slowing, nearly coming to a halt. The final blow sent shockwaves through my entire body. An explosion of fire burst near my eyes, sending me through a blinding whiteness.

"Son. Son. Lyle? I need you to wake up. Can you hear me? Open your eyes, please."

I felt a light tap against my cheek, alarming my senses, shooting my eyes open.

"Oh, I didn't mean to alarm you. I just ... well ... there are some things we need to discuss. Now, if you will. Please get changed and meet me down in the dining room. Take your time getting ready. But when you are, please meet me down there, understand?"

Charles's eyebrows lifted in unison, his forehead crinkling, but his eyes dropped in shame. He couldn't meet my stare. He gently pressed his palm onto my chest, glanced up at me, pressing his lips together, before returning his gaze to the floor and walking out of the room. There was something wrong. Something uneasy about the way he held his hand on my chest. Charles was a man of a deep and intensely dark stare. He never cowered from meeting a man eye to eye. In meetings and negotiations, this was his key factor for winning out. His poker face never faltered and he never relented in his eyes.

His words chimed in, sending me into an apprehensive mood. "Always watch the eyes, Lyle. They will tell you what words will not. What they cannot. The mouth will lie, but the eyes never will. They are the soul to the person. Watch them, and you will always know their next move. I promise."

I wasn't sure what Charles's next move was, but deep within me, I knew it wasn't good. I quickly changed, putting on my best suit and shoes. My mind fell to this outfit, a deep striking feeling telling me this would be the last time I would wear it. Standing before the mirror, I combed my hair and tied my tie. I stood there for some time, looking inward at myself. Not in vanity, not at my reflection, but at an overview of who I had become. The boy who had holes in his socks, shoes with soles that fell apart consistently, and smelled like dirt is wearing tailored suits, leather boots, and fragrances that I cannot pronounce. How did I end up here?

And this house . . . so exquisite, grandiose, and well-kept. I wish Clara could have seen this. She would have enjoyed listening to sonata's in the morning and dancing throughout the countless rooms on the glistening wooden floors. I had my own room with an actual bathroom, not an outhouse. Real running water to shower and bathe as I please. The money, the riches, all the fine dining I could take. All of it because of one man: Charles. Where would I be without him?

Does he feel I am ungrateful for what he has bestowed upon me? Is this it? I must tell him. I must make my gratitude known.

Taking a deep inhale, I walked toward the doorway but stopped as I reached the outside, turning back to take a look at my room. I stood there, taking in the view, engraining it in my brain. The red satin sheets, the large-scale windows pouring in generous amounts of natural light, and the delicately handcrafted oak bedframe. My eyes lingered on each item, without a reason, finally turning from the room, taking to the stairs. The atmosphere around me fell quiet, everything slowed. My steps thudded against the wooden steps, feeling as if I was in a freeze-frame, the clock barely ticking.

"Ah! Lyle, thank you for coming. Please, please sit."

Charles motioned to the pulled out chair at the opposite end of the dining table. Even though it was usually just him and I, with the exception of occasional guests, there laid, under the gaudy crystal chandelier, an eight person oak table. I leerily strolled to the seat, never taking my eyes from his. But still, he could not look me in the eyes. With my hand resting on the top of the chair, I stood, waiting for him to sit as well. He was standing at the head of the table, chair pulled back, papers sprawled out over the table.

"Sit. Please." His hand raised in the air.

"What is this pertaining to, Charles?" I stood there, perplexed.

"It would be better if we could speak sitting, please."

"It would be better if you told me what in the hell is going on here." I pointed toward the mess on the table. "Financial disclosures. What is this? What? You don't trust—"

"I said sit, damnit!" He pounded his fist against the table, cutting me off.

It was rare to see him in such an angered state. This was very unlike Charles. Cooler heads always prevailed with him. Worry and dread built in my bones. But I wasn't ready to sit. I needed to know. Something was off, something was wrong.

"Damnit, Lyle! Why do you have to always be so Goddamn stubborn? Why can't you just do what you are told?"

"This is much more than me sitting. Go on, Charles. What did you bring me down here to say? Go on with it!" I persisted.

He finally looked up at me, his eyes reddened and puffy.

"Lyle, the police will be here in one hour. I asked them to give me some time with you before they came. But they will be here. They will be here for you."

"What?"

"Yes, I'm sorry. But I thought you should know."

"You called the police? Why—What exactly should I know? Is this, is this *you*?"

Taking a deep and audible sigh, he shook his head, dropping his eyes to the table.

"Do you see these here? These, these right here. These are all of my clients. Their finances, their disclosures, addresses, family members, all of it. Right here." He pressed his index finger into the sheets of paper.

"Yes?" I wasn't sure where he was going with this.

"This, these people, they are my livelihood. My business. My life. My *legacy*. As you know, I came from nothing. This. All of this right here, this home. The home you rest your head in, my home. All of this was because of me. *My hard work.* My clients are all I have. They are the essence of my existence. If I lost them, son, I'd lose everything."

His tone grew somber. But the words were building up to the crescendo he was aiming to surprise me with.

"I understand, Ch—"

"Do you Lyle? Do you really? You were nothing but a punk kid on the street eating from trash bins when I took pity on you." His hand lifted up, motioning to point before he thought the better of it. "And look at you now. Sharp tailored suits. Leather boots. Women eating out of your hand. The finest dining options. Money raining down. And you manage to screw it all up? To fuck with my business? To fuck with me? Is this how you treat the man who raised you as his own? Who honored and took care of you? Is this what you have become? You owe me, boy! I *made you*!"

"Charles, I am not following. What is this that you speak of? I would never try to hurt your business. I am grateful for the life you have given me, for all of this."

"As you Goddamn should."

He sighed, leaning into the back of the chair before collapsing in the seat.

"I told you early on, anything, *anyone*, who tries to take from you, to take from your next meal, punch back. *Always*. Lyle, You are bad for my business. All of it. The murders. Stealing their money afterward. I can't have it. Clearly. I have clients threatening me from coast to coast. My name is being dragged through the Goddamn streets because of you."

Charles buried his head in his hands, rubbing against the back of his neck.

"How did you . . .?"

"What? How did I know? It's my Goddamn job to know. I know every man you have killed, every dollar you have stolen, and every fucking cent you have spent. My boy, I have had an eye on you from the moment I took you in."

"If you knew . . . . why didn't you stop me?"

My legs grew weak, prompting me to scoot into the chair, my arms leaning onto the table.

"I ask myself this every day . . . I saw something in you. Something that even you didn't see in yourself. The possibilities. The future. All fucking wasted."

He roared before palming his hands against the table, attempting to calm himself.

"Even though I may treat you like one, you are not my blood. You are not of me. You never will be. For the better. You kill? For what? For fun? For money? I have all you could ever want, tell me. Tell me, boy. Why? Because I cannot, for the life of me, seem to figure it out."

"Charles ... I ..."

His head carefully lifted revealing a lone tear parading down his left cheek. He quickly wiped the back of his hand to rid of it.

"You are no son of mine. You are *nothing*. This is me punching back." Charles slammed his fist abruptly against the table. The impact was nearly too much for him as he had to tend to his hand as he continued to speak. "Lyle, the men you killed ... those were friends of mine. Men of astronomical wealth. Wealth that you and I can only dream of. Generations of money and family lineages of wealth. These people ... they have made me wildly rich. And they were loyal, Goddamn you! Do you know how hard it is to find loyal clients in this business? We hide money for Christ's sake, they are crooked already. But yet they stay. Stayed with me all these years. And now word has spread, people are demanding new representation, my firm is in shambles. The IRS will be at my door soon. All of this, because of *you*."

"Charles, you don't know these men. The sick and twisted things they did ... These are not good men. They are—"

"What? Monsters? Is this what you were going to say? A Goddamn monster? What does that make you?"

His echoes bounced through the wallpapered walls, attacking me from multiple directions. He could see he opened a wound, so he dug even deeper.

"And, how would you know what a good man was? You are a Goddamn murdering thief! A bum. That's how you started as and that's how you will end. You are nothing to me, ya hear? Fucking nothing!"

Those words stung deeply into my chest. He was no longer throwing softballs but low blows. He was turning the curve, aiming to hit.

"Nonsense! How could you say any of this? After everything? After everything we have been through?" I let the words sit in the air, but he turned his scowling face from me. My fists balled with emotion threatening to pour out of me. "These vile men. Putrid scum! Abusers. Torturers. Masochists. Children, women, all victimized, humiliated, damaged, forever. How could you stand by this? Standing by them makes you just the same. I will not apologize, no. They deserved what they had coming to them! If it wasn't me . . . they were dead anyways."

"Lyle, you just don't seem to understand. There is no good, there is no bad. People just *are*. It is not my business to judge these men, only to make a better life for me. And I, so kindly, helped you as well. You are lost in the black and white representation. There is no such thing. Even with you. You fancy yourself some white knight riding in here on a steed preaching morality when you kill? Who in the fuck do you think you are? These *men*, they have their fetishes . . . I don't approve, but it is not my concern. My only concern is my money. My money is my life. And you, boy, have just stepped into a world you cannot imagine." His face lifted to the wall, cold as stone. "Really, I am doing you a service, Lyle. A kindness after all you have done against me. Turning you into the police is the kind path. It is the one that allows you another day of breath. What you don't understand, those men out there, their goons, they know all about you, and they want you dead. They want *me* dead. Word spreads quickly here, an untamed wildfire. Now they are coming to put you out. You are the cancer they never expected. Inheritances . . . squandered. Tainting old money is the first step to getting shot! I should hand you over to them. Oh, the *things* they want to do to you." He stood from the chair, turning into the window behind him, looking through the curtains. His hands clasped tightly behind his back.

"But I still care for you. Something still tying myself to you. I cannot shake it. I try, of course, but, alas, it remains. *You* were what I was most proud of. But now . . ."— he drifted near me, laying his hand on top of my shoulder—"now, you are dead to me."

The dagger I had been waiting for sailed through the air, piercing into my heart. I could feel a lump settling at the back of my throat. My intentions were never to hurt Charles. I cannot help who I am. Who I had become. I tried desperately to fight against the tides of fury and anger. But it was a losing battle. I would see myself in those children, even the women. The vulnerable. I couldn't fathom how these men, who had everything, could enjoy inflicting so much terror on those below them.

"I feel no remorse for what I have done. I will apologize for nothing. My heart will never lay heavy. The only sorrow I have, it lies with you. I wish it didn't have to become what it is now. I never meant for this to happen. You were the man I needed as a father. In my case, time just didn't seem to heal all wounds. My wish is if I would have met you sooner . . . my life may have been different. This, this all could have been different."

His eyes turned to mine, locking fiercely to each other's. My hand reached up to his, grasping it intently.

"I will miss you, Charles. I loved you. And I am sorry . . ."

His panicked eyes filled with desperation as I bolted from my seat, tightening my fingers around his neck. Charles tried to buck against me, but my strength overpowered him, his aging body slumbering down into the floor. His attempts to fight against me only worked to weaken himself. With a tear dripping from my eye, I curled my fingers in tighter, my mind recounting every word he had spoken. His clawing hands scratching against my face and neck deepened the rage fighting inside me. I was no longer me. That euphoria was quickly taking over. *IT* was in control. Quick ragged gasps exerted from his throat as his once galivanting heart slowed in tempo.

I could feel the muscles in my own neck tense while the veins in my hand were nearly protruding. My heart lumped violently across my chest. My thoughts were quieted, only focusing on the moment. I watched eagerly as the life in his eyes slowly fainted away. The candle's wick was near its final burning end. With his face morphing into a sickening color, I felt his final staggered breath, a quickened gasp sending his body into a stiffened position. The candle had finally been blown out.

Sitting back, my wide grip loosened from his neck to reveal perfect red imprints burned into it. My eyes stared blankly at him, allowing the euphoria to rise into me, masking me into its eruption. The clarity of what I had just done was unbeknownst to me in this moment. He was not Charles, but a man, a stranger, lying dormant beneath my feet.

My head fell back and my eyes rolled into me. I could feel a smile etching into my face as I inhaled deeply, basking in the moment.

But the vivid memories of Charles and I projected into my mind, dancing from happy memory to happy memory. They replayed in order, with my smiles clearly in focus. Charles teaching me how to tie my first tie, polish my shoes, etiquette lessons, walking with me to my first day of higher education, so cheerfully praising me at my graduation, my first day at the law office, our time at the operas, sonatas, every dinner we had, all of it, hauntingly replayed.

My throat tightened, as if I, too, was being strangled, while my gut wrenched. I could feel a wave of sorrow rising within me. Something I had never felt after a kill. A loud sob escaped my lips, surprising even me. My quivering hands lifted to cover my mouth just as a flood of tears burst through my closed eyes. The wailing sent echoes through the vaulted ceilings. My soul poured from my eyes into my hands.

I peeled back my weighted eyelids, blinking audibly, allowing the watering eyes to adjust. A deep ocean blue hue was fixed on me from the corner of the room. The walls lined with concrete, the heavy metal door was open allowing the hallway's light to breach onto my face, exposing me. I quickly surveyed the room. Dr. Holmes's blood splattered body pressed into the floor with only his head holding him up, leaning into the wall. His former blue eyes were blanketed in white. Tommy's body was scattered across the room, and the *man* with no name lay broken in the distance.

The creature lingered his way toward me on all fours. Not a word was said, but the moment was clear. There was no way out. Armageddon has come. I had relived all I needed to; everything was completed. My spirit steered between fighting for another chance or sitting into the inevitability. A gust of frosty wind breezed around me. My mouth opened, tasting the chill of a winter storm. My legs beckoned me to stand, somehow regaining their strength and mobility. I adhered to its call, slowly rising to my feet, eyes watching the looming threat coming before me.

The creature felt worlds away, yet its descent drew nearer. Whispering lowly to myself, I vowed to fight against this darkening. Every piece of me, of what I had left, moved toward this entity. We were set to clash. Even if it meant meeting my end, this darkness would not win out. For too long

I had allowed it to cloud my mind, terrifying me into submission. Images of terror, contrived or in reality, the pleasure of my fear will not last. I will not go quietly.

The feeling of impending dread lifted, delving into a chaotic beauty. My lips pursed slightly and my eyes narrowed in on the creature. But his image slowly morphed, stopping me dead in my tracks. A misty fog danced up my legs and a crisp chilly wind patted me down. I turned in a circle, circumventing my area, watching it morph into something entirely new, different.

My head cocked to the right, aghast to see a familiar street corner. I had returned to the streets of New York, situated on the corner. A street lamp from the adjacent street corner flickered on, revealing a familiar, lonely face. It was me.

There I stood under a street lamp on a busy street, unperturbed by the busy world carrying on around me, searching through the crowded faces. Eagerly expecting, as if he had been waiting for some time. My other-self caught whim of my imminent arrival, rallying me to come over, hands waving in the air, a true and meaningful smile radiating from my face. The sun lifted from the clouds, dancing across my face, bathing me in its warmth. We both lifted our heads to the sky, taking it in, it all in.

Bolts of pressure attempted to phase me, but my other-self continued to wave me forward. The sounds of gunshots in the distance faded as a serenely lovely melody drifted through my ears. I dared not to look down but could feel warm liquid flowing down my chest. But the exuberant energy poured from my other-self into me, promising me more energy to finish my journey. More pressing bolts of pressure littered across my body, but it no longer mattered. I had arrived. The other-me lifted his hands to place on my shoulders, mouthing inaudible congratulatory words. The words whispered into my soul, sending chills of elation and peace. I had never felt so free.

The chains violently clanked against the floor, finally freeing me from their bondage. All falling in unison. I let out a deep exhale, looking to the sky, basking in the warmth of the radiating sun. All of the pain and the sorrow freed itself from my soul as I descended into a world of peace.

ABOUT THE AUTHOR

TALESA JARAMILLO WAS BORN AND raised in the city of Pueblo in the beautiful state of Colorado. Now living in Arizona, Talesa is pursuing her master's degree and enjoys engaging in various hobbies outside of writing, including hiking and Muay Thai. Her interest in writing began at a young age when she won a citywide scary story contest. *Mind of the Madness* is Talesa's first book, further establishing her in the horror/thriller genre.

www.ingramcontent.com/pod-product-compliance
Lightning Source LLC
Chambersburg PA
CBHW032120170626
46808CB00006B/2026